"There's not many who'd want to be mistaken for a back-shooting killer," the deputy growled.

"I said somebody mistook me for Bill Longley," the blond Texan countered. "Not Wyatt Earp."

"Don't you mean-mouth Mr. Earp, you god-damned beefhead!" Martin spat out, grabbing for the revolver in his right side holster.

At the same time, Waco's hands made a blurring motion, as his staghorn-handled Colt Artillery Model Peacemakers rose above the lips of their respective holsters. To the accompaniment of a clicking, as the hammers were thumbed back to the fully cocked position, the five-and-a-half-inch barrels turned forward. Seeming far larger than their caliber of .45 of an inch, the muzzles were pointed directly at the suddenly shocked and paling face of the deputy.

A concerted gasp arose from the crowd. Like the deputy, every man present knew they had just witnessed a superlative exhibition of gun handling. There was, however, one very important difference from the point of view of the crowd and that of Martin.

While the interest of the onlookers was merely academic, the deputy knew he had never been in greater peril.

Books by J.T. Edson

WACO'S BADGE
TEXAS KILLERS
COLD DECK, HOT LEAD

WACO'S
BADGE

J.T. EDSON

HarperTorch
An Imprint of HarperCollinsPublishers

This is a work of fiction. Names, characters, places, and incidents are products of the author's imagination or are used fictitiously and are not to be construed as real. Any resemblance to actual events, locales, organizations, or persons, living or dead, is entirely coincidental.

HARPERTORCH
An Imprint of HarperCollins*Publishers*
10 East 53rd Street
New York, New York 10022-5299

First HarperTorch paperback printing: April 2005

HarperCollins®, HarperTorch™, and ❦ ™ are trademarks of HarperCollins Publishers Inc.

Printed in the United States of America

Visit HarperTorch on the World Wide Web at www.harpercollins.com

10 9 8 7 6 5 4 3 2 1

*For Joan's daughter, Caroline,
despite her driving as far with a six iron
as I can with a five.*

Author's Note

Although one version of the events recorded herein appeared as Case One, "The Set-Up," *Sagerbrush Sleuth*, we did not at that time have access to the full details. These have now been made available to us by Alvin Dustine "Cap" Fog and, where information regarding the participation of Belle Starr is concerned, Andrew Mark "Big Andy" Counter, along with permission to reproduce them.

We realize that, in our present "permissive" society, we could include the actual profanities used by various people who appear in this volume, but we do not concede a spurious desire to produce "realism" is a valid reason for doing so.

As we refuse to pander to the current "trendy" employment of the metric system, unless we are referring to the calibres appropriate to various weapons—e.g. Luger 9mm—we will continue to employ miles, yards, feet, inches, pounds and ounces when referring to measurements and weights.

Lastly, to save our "old hands" from repetition and for the benefit of new readers, we are giving details of the background and special qualifications of Waco in Appendix One.

> J.T. Edson,
> Active Member, Western Writers of America
> Melton Mowbray,
> Leics.
> England

WACO'S BADGE

Chapter 1

ONE HELL OF AN EDGE

❦ ❦

DURING THE MID-1800S THERE WERE A NUMBER OF ways by which people, their property, or mail could be transported across the vast and ever changing terrain between the Mississippi River and the Pacific shore of the United States of America. One could travel on horseback, leading pack animals. Scorning such a new fangled idea as the wheel, an Indian brave-heart warrior had his squaw haul his belongings on a two pole *travois* attached to her mount.

Not that one was compelled to make a journey sitting astride a saddle. On some Western rivers such as the Rio Grande, steamboats—although smaller and less majestic than the fabled "side-wheelers" of the

Big Muddy—could be found. Already the railroad had linked the East and West Coasts and spur lines were spreading like the strands of a spider's web. For all that, such were the enormous areas involved, considerable distances remained inaccessible to the "iron horse" and must be traversed by some other form of wheeled vehicle.

Prior to the development of the internal combustion engine, with the exception of the railroad, the fastest form of public transport was the stagecoach. No other means of travelling had the glamor, nor received so much dramatic coverage in the sensational newspapers and magazines of the day. While goods in bulk could not be carried, such a vehicle served to deliver passengers, their smaller belongings and the United States' mails to regions where, as yet, the railroads had not reached.[1]

The stagecoach as a form of public transport had not been invented in the United States, versions of it having been operating in most European countries since at least the seventeenth century. However, it had soon become apparent that the heavy and lum-

---

1. The idea of having mail carried by stagecoach instead of on horseback is said to have been originated in England early in the eighteenth century by John Palmer, manager of the Orchard Street Theater, Bath. As Mrs. Sarah Siddons—the greatest actress of the period—frequently had to appear in Drury Lane, London, and at Bath and Bristol in the same week, seeking to make travelling easier for her, he persuaded the great statesman, William Pitt, to have the Royal Mails delivered by stagecoach between the towns on a daily basis. The idea proved so popular and efficient, it spread throughout the United Kingdom and was eventually copied by other countries. J.T.E.

bering vehicles brought over from the "old countries" during the Colonial period were not suitable for the conditions which prevailed in the "New World." Therefore, as befited a lusty, bustling, expanding and innovative young nation, in which fresh thought and creative notions were encouraged instead of being repressed, men had sought to make improvements.

Not merely *sought,* in fact, but *achieved*!

"Yankee" designers, generally in the North-Eastern section of the country—New Hampshire, Maine, Vermont, Connecticut, Rhode Island and Massachusetts—known as "New England," had brought the stagecoach to such a peak of perfection that the various improvements were already being copied throughout the rest of the world.

The stagecoach wending its way along the winding trail through the hilly country between Phoenix and Tucson, about two miles from the boundary of Pinal and Pima Counties, was a typical example of the way in which such vehicles had been developed.

Set on "dished" wheels which were larger at the rear than in front,[2] weighing three thousand pounds and capable of carrying a four thousand pound load, the coach was structurally powerful without being in any way cumbersome. Its woodwork was choicest hickory and, apart from brass trimming, its metal was all steel, with axles fourteen inches long and two

2. The purpose of "dished" wheels is described in: *THE WHIP AND THE WAR LANCE.* J.T.E.

and a half inches thick.[3] Inside, the cushions were built over coiled steel springs, padded with horsehair and, although it had become somewhat scuffed by much use, the seats were covered with the very best available calf leather. Some further comfort for the passengers was obtained by having the body swung upon leather "thorough-braces"; long, heavy straps rove through stout steel stanchions lifting above the front and rear axles, left and right. In addition, layer upon layer of "live" leather created a velvety, hammock-like swing and a cushioning to the body that has scarcely been equalled even by the best modern springing in motor vehicles.

Entrance to the stagecoach was via the doorways at the sides, with hanging steel step plates as an aid to boarding. Although the early models used in the East had had glass in the doors and small quarter windows in the frames on each side, this had proved impractical on the far from smooth and carefully laid roads west of the Big Muddy. Instead, the unglazed windows beside the front and rear seats were protected by canvas curtains. These rolled up and down upon a stout slat, being secured by eyes and turnbuttons when down, or held in a rolled-up position by leather straps.

Inside, two of the three seats faced forward and a third to the rear. The center seat could be lowered to form a bed and, if there were not too many passen-

---

3. See: *Paragraph Three, AUTHOR'S NOTE.* J.T.E.

gers, the occupants could lie down to rest as the coach rocked along. Each seat was sufficiently spacious to accept three normal sized people without too much crowding. As there was provision for three more seats on the roof—which was covered with the very heaviest of painted waterproof duck, the coach could offer transportation for twelve to fifteen passengers in reasonable comfort and had, on rare occasions, packed in as many as twenty-four. There were leather "tug" straps on each side, to which those sitting next to the windows could cling if necessary. As the internal seats were fairly close together, whoever was on the front seat and facing to the rear had to "dovetail" his legs—one name for the practice—with those of the forward-facing occupants in the center. It was an arrangement which, at least openly, did not meet with the approbation of the "good" ladies of the period.

As was frequently the case, the coach was brightly painted in red, gold and yellow. The body was ribbed and panelled. It had floral and vine patterns on the side panels and the doors were inscribed with the words, "PHOENIX to TUCSON" and, as it travelled to and from the capital city of the territory, the paintwork was kept fresh despite generally being coated with dust or mud dependent upon the time of the year. Because the bottom of the vehicle curved like a boat, the side ribs came to a prow-like point beneath the seat of the driver—under which was announced, somewhat prematurely, "ARIZONA STATE STAGE

LINE, Coach Three"—and ended in a blunter "stern" at the rear.

In the European type of vehicle from which the American "Concord" stagecoaches evolved,[4] the makers having little concern for the comfort and well being of even so important an employee as the driver, the "box" serving as his seat was part of the chassis. Brought up in the concept that "all men are born equal," such disinterest was unacceptable in the United States. Therefore, also as an aid to greater efficiency, the American manufacturers had attached the seat for the driver to the front of the body, with its top forming a shoulder high rest for his back and making his demanding task somewhat less tiring. Furthermore, unlike his European predecessors, in this way he too received the benefit of the excellent springing offered by the thoroughbracing.

Sitting at the right side of the box, where a powerful foot brake was provided, the driver was some six feet from the ground. As was the case with the armed man who generally rode beside him, this provided all round visibility of a high order. Directly beneath their shelf-like seat, a small compartment was supplied in which such valuables as a strongbox or the mail sacks could be carried. Beneath this was a larger, leather-shrouded "boot" for baggage. However,

---

4. During the 1820s, manufacturers in the town of Concord, New Hampshire—notably Abbott, Downing & Co.—had proved the quality of their stagecoaches to the point where their superlative designs had become the final word for such vehicles everywhere in the world. J.T.E.

heavier items within reason were transported on a hinged platform—also provided with a protective leather, or canvas, hood—supported by chains, at the rear of the coach. If these two should prove insufficient and no passengers were up there, railings around the top offered space for still more luggage.

Being drawn in this particular instance by six horses, in three teams of two, to control such a vehicle called for great skill. A pair of leather reins came back to the expert hands of the driver from each of the teams and manipulating the "ribbons" was no mean feat. It was simplified to a certain extent by each rein being split at the forward end. The separated ends of the right rein was linked to the off side of each horse's jaw and those of the left to the near side. By this means, a single pull directed both animals of the team. For all that, driving a stagecoach was hardly a task for the uninitiated.[5]

Six foot tall, lean and oak brown from long exposure to the elements, at forty-nine, Walter Tract was a driver of some ten years' experience. Unlike some of his contemporaries, he did not effect flamboyant dress and mannerisms to indicate he was a highly skilled workman. His attire was little different from that of a working cowhand, except that his well worn Levi's pants were tucked into blunt toed boots with low heels. A walnut handled Colt Civilian Model

---

5. How an uninitiated person, albeit one with considerable experience in handling a heavy freight wagon, coped when compelled by circumstances to drive a stagecoach is told in: *CALAMITY SPELLS TROUBLE.* J.T.E.

Peacemaker rode in the cross draw holster on the left side of his gunbelt,[6] but in the event of trouble he relied more upon the man at his left side than his own ability with the weapon.

Matching the driver in height, build and depth of tanning, Benjamin Eckland was a few years younger. He too was dressed in the style of a cowhand, which indeed he had been before taking on the—on the surface—easier occupation of "shotgun messenger." There was something dour about him which suggested he would stand no nonsense and was an asset in his chosen line of work. However, although his *buscadero* gunbelt supported two wooden butted Colt Cavalry Peacemakers in its fast draw holsters and he was nursing a Greener twin barrelled ten gauge shotgun, the tubes only twenty inches in length, he had nothing of the swaggering frontier gun fighter frequently described with great relish in the "blood and thunder" literature which found as large a market in the West as back East. Rather he was a calm, competent guard who took no unnecessary chances in the performance of his duty. This did not imply he was cowardly. He had broken up an attack by Apaches and, when they tried to carry out a poorly planned hold up, left a gang of would-be stagecoach robbers with one dead and three wounded.

"Just what the hell is this country coming to,

6. Information regarding the various models of the Colt Model P "Single Action Army" revolver, known as "the Peacemaker" can be found in: *Footnote 3, APPENDIX ONE*. J.T.E.

Ben?" Tract inquired, breaking the silence—as far as conversation went—which had endured since leaving the last way station after having changed horses. "A sheriff takes a posse after and catches a bunch of god-damned owlhoots who've robbed a bank in his bailiwick and now some 'mother-something'[7] fancy law wrangler from back East makes the court turn 'em loose because he went over his county line and grabbed 'em."

"Don't seem at all right to me, Walt, and that's a living fact," Eckland replied, the topic currently arousing much interest and heated discussion throughout the whole of Arizona Territory. "More 'specially seeing's how said fancy law wrangler from back East is threatening to sue the sheriff and his county for him doing same."

"You're *joshing* me, Ben!" the driver asserted, knowing his companion had a droll sense of humor beneath the dour exterior.

"I only wish I *was*," the guard replied grimly. "Lanky back to the way station told me about it. He got the word from a whiskey drummer's passed through yesterday. Seems like the law wrangler's let on as he's ready and willing to fight the case all the way clear up to the Supreme Court of these here United States should it 'come necessary.' "

"But how the shit can he figure's how he's got him a god-damned case to fight?"

---

7. See: *Paragraph Two, AUTHOR'S NOTE.* J.T.E.

"Allows the sheriff didn't have no legal jurisdiction in the county where he took those owlhoot sons-of-bitches. Which being, they was abdu—abduct—some such fancy law wrangling word, anyways—again' their will and same's against the Constitution of the good old U.S. of A."

"God damn it all!" Tract protested, despite being aware that a sheriff technically had authority only in the county by which he was elected to the office. "That *can't* be the legal law?"

"Said fancy law wrangler from back East allows it to be," Eckland said dryly, but with an underlying bitterness and anger which was all too apparent to anybody who knew him as well as the other man on the box. "And, should it be so, that gives every god-damned owlhoot in this whole country one hell of an edge over the law. All he'll have to do is go across a county, or State line, and the peace officers who're after him won't be able to follow."

"I bet the sheriff's right now wishing he'd made wolf bait of every last son-of-a-bitch of that gang instead of fetching them in," Tract declared, sharing his companion's appreciation of the situation and equally perturbed by the thought of how criminals could profit out of the successful outcome—from the point of view of the Eastern lawyer—of the case. "Fact being, seeing what he could turn loose should he win, somebody should do it to that 'mother—'!"

The angry tirade came to an abrupt halt!

Despite the strength of his feelings on the subject

being discussed, the driver had instinctively kept his attention upon the trail ahead. Selected as offering the easiest going through the hilly terrain, it wound in a serpentine fashion across the side of the sloping ground. Although visibility ahead was somewhat restricted, he had seen something which he considered to be of greater importance than what he was saying.

A riderless horse, its one-piece reins suspended across its neck, was running around the bend which the stagecoach was approaching!

To a person raised in the East, such a sight would have been interesting without arousing too much concern!

Anywhere on the vast open ranges west of the Mississippi River, however, there was nothing more disturbing than a horse running with an empty saddle!

In that sparsely occupied and vast land, where innumerable natural hazards lurked—even discounting the various perils created by hostile human beings—to be left afoot suggested a vastly greater danger than could be envisaged by people in the more densely populated and civilized East!

Therefore, interested as he had been in the activities of the Eastern lawyer, the driver put the matter from his mind as soon as the riderless horse came into view!

Keeping a watch on his surroundings just as instinctively while talking, Eckland also forgot the conversation when the animal made its appearance.

Such was the nature of the terrain currently being

traversed by the stagecoach, their point of vantage on the box notwithstanding, neither Tract nor the shotgun messenger could satisfy their curiosity concerning the person who had lost the horse. Nor, as far as they could hear, was whoever had been dislodged from its back giving any indication of being close by. If he was able, when left in such an unsatisfactory situation, a cowhand would have raised the already traditional cry of, "Catch my saddle!,"[8] in the hope of somebody being near enough to hear and comply. Of course, he might be too badly injured to speak. Or he might be too far away for his voice to have reached the stagecoach. He might, in fact, not even be a cowhand.

The latter was a distinct possibility!

Without the need to guide his actions consciously, Eckland was studying the horse. A washy bay gelding of about fourteen hands and with no particularly distinguishing marks, it was not an impressive creature. Rather the opposite, in fact. For all that, there were a few indications to his range-wise eyes which led him to assume the absent rider was not a cowhand. Instead of the more general "split end" variety, its reins were in a single piece. The former were more favored in the West—particularly by cowhands—as, many horses being trained to stand still when they were

---

8. In all probability, the horse from which a cowhand was thrown, or otherwise dislodged, belonged to the rancher by whom he was currently hired. On the other hand, the saddle was generally his personal and most important item of property: hence the way in which the request for assistance was worded. J.T.E.

dangling free, it meant that the dropped reins—if one was thrown—soon caused the animal to come to a stop. Single girthed and "apple" horned, the saddle was a normal enough rig for the area. There was, however, no coiled lariat strapped to the horn and a cowhand was rarely without such an important tool of his trade. That there were neither blankets nor a bed roll attached to the cantle of the saddle was less informative. Their absence indicated the dislodged rider was not too far from some form of accommodation.

Lacking any positive information regarding the person from whom the horse had escaped, the two men on the box felt it incumbent upon them to take precautions. While Tract was causing his team to slow down, but was equally ready to goad them to increased speed should this be called for, Ekland was easing the Greener into a position of greater readiness and preparing to draw its hammers to the fully cocked position. Even if the horse had not swerved aside to run away at an angle on seeing them, they were aware of their duty to the passengers, and neither would have considered stopping and trying to catch the bay. It might, each realized, have been released to cause this to happen so a hold up could take place. If this was not the case, however, the range-bred animal would return to the place it regarded as its home and was unlikely to be lost.

Not until they were going around the bend were the men able to obtain at least one answer to their questions!

Taking in the sight which met their gaze, the driver and the guard regarded it with mingled emotions!

Sprawled on her back, unmoving in the center of the trail was a good looking and shapely young woman. On landing, she had lost the low crowned, wide brimmed black Spanish style hat she had been wearing and her formerly neat blonde hair was dishevelled. The white blouse she had on beneath a brown bolero jacket had burst open, allowing one bare and sizeable breast to be thrust into view. Rucked up, her doeskin divided skirt displayed two well curved legs encased in black stockings to just above knee level and a pair of black riding boots. Although brown leather gauntlets covered her hands and concealed any indication of her marital status, they were empty.

Instinctively, Tract began to haul back on the ribbons and used his right foot to apply the brake. Already having been slowed down, the well trained horses had no difficulty in responding to his verbal and physical demands for them to stop.

Skilled at his work, Eckland gazed carefully about him as the vehicle was being brought to a halt. There were many places close by where men could be concealed and at least three locations within half a mile were large enough to hide several horses. However, despite the scrutiny to which he subjected all of them, he could detect no trace of any being occupied. For all that, despite there being a beautiful young woman lying in front of the stagecoach, he remained wary and kept a grip upon his shotgun.

"Is something wrong?" called a voice with a carrying and bombastic New England tone.

"Nothing to worry about, Senator," the driver replied, looking around to where a face reddened by the sun, with an expression suggesting pomposity and framed by a mass of white hair, was peering up at him through the uncovered off side rear window. "Could be there's been an accident. Just stay put inside, all of you, and Ben 'n' me'll 'tend to things."

As Tract was returning his attention to the trail ahead, noticing in passing that Eckland was still holding the shotgun and looking around, the young woman stirred. Slowly and with a suggestion of being in considerable pain, placing her hands flat on the ground as an aid to moving, she began to raise her head and shoulders. Before she could attain a sitting position, it seemed the effort had proved too much for her. Giving a groan, she collapsed to lie supine and unmoving once more.

"Looks like she's hurt bad, Ben!" the driver assessed.

"I'll go along with you on that, Walt," the guard conceded, but he swung another sweeping gaze around the halted stagecoach.

"Maybe you'd best go take a look-see," Tract suggested, after he too had glanced at the surrounding terrain and seen nothing to arouse his suspicions. Despite his concern over the possibility that the woman might be seriously injured, he approved of the caution being displayed by his companion and went on, "I'll keep watch while you're doing it."

"Whichever way you want it, *amigo*," Eckland assented, leaning the Greener against the seat where it would be within easy reach of the driver. His voice remained dour as he went on, "Then, should we get throwed down on by owlhoots, I'll lay all the blame on lil old you."

"You would've anyways," Tract claimed.

There was, the guard told himself silently as he was dropping to the ground and approaching the motionless figure, no reason why he should expect trouble!

In accordance with the policy of the Arizona State Stage Line, Eckland had been informed before leaving the depot at Phoenix that the strongbox contained nothing a criminal would regard as being negotiable and, therefore, worth trying to steal. Nor, to the best of his knowledge, was any of the four passengers carrying such a large sum of money, or quantity of other valuables, as to offer an inducement for a gang of outlaws to plan a hold up using the attractive young woman and her "lost" horse as a decoy. He had taken his precautions against such an eventuality merely as a matter of routine and he had seen nothing during his examination of the immediate vicinity of the stagecoach to suggest that robbers were lurking ready to pounce.

Yet, for all his apparently comforting summations, the shotgun messenger felt vaguely uneasy!

Although Eckland could not decide what it might be, there was something about the situation he found disturbing and puzzling!

The presence of the woman was certainly out of the ordinary!

While the attire of the blonde was that of a "good" woman and designed for riding on horseback, the guard wondered how she came to be in the vicinity. Although he and the driver were new to the "run," to the best of his knowledge the nearest ranch house was some ten miles away. The towns of Red Rock and Marana, respectively in Pinal and Pima Counties, were closer and connected by the trail which the stagecoach was using. It was possible she could be going from one to the other for some reason. Certainly the horse he had seen running away was of a quality more generally offered for rent from the livery barns of such small communities than in the *remuda* of a ranch.

What struck Eckland as most unusual was that, to all appearances, the woman had been making the journey alone!

Still plagued by his misgivings, the guard crouched and began to bend over the blonde. She showed no visible signs of injury, but he knew this did not preclude the possibility of her having sustained damage of some kind as a result of being thrown from the horse. He had seen sufficient accidents of that nature to be aware of how serious the results could be.

Regardless of his concern for her well being, Eckland could not prevent his gaze from turning to the exposed and bare breast. Full and firm, the nipple rising in a prominent brown mound above the white flesh, it was a sight to distract any normal man. However, even as he was looking, he was struck by a thought. From all he had heard and what experience led him to assume was the case, "good" women invariably wore undergarments of some kind beneath their outer clothing, no matter how warm the weather. As far as he could see, which was a considerable distance, the blonde was not wearing anything to waist level under the open white blouse.

Even as the shotgun messenger was starting to contemplate the possibilities suggested by the absence of undergarments, the woman opened her eyes!

There was an expression of mockery in the gaze of the blonde as, thrusting herself rapidly into a sitting position, she flung a handful of sandy soil into Eckland's face!

Chapter 2

WHY DON'T YOU *TELL* THEM WHO I AM

~~~

AS HE SAW THE CHANGE COME OVER THE WOMAN, RE-alizing that he had been tricked after all, Benjamin Eckland's instincts as a shotgun messenger took over. Silently cursing himself for having fallen into a trap, which no man could have sprung upon him, he began to straighten up with his right hand dipping toward the butt of the holstered off side Colt Cavalry Peacemaker. Thrown with considerable force, the impact of the gritty grains against his features caused him to rise much faster than he had intended and to lose his balance. What was more, partially blinded by the unexpected attack, he fumbled his draw.

The guard was not granted an opportunity to clear his vision, nor to regain control of his movements!

Thrusting herself upward, with a speed and ease of motion which removed all indication of her having sustained an injury when "losing" the horse, the blonde continued to respond swiftly and effectively. As soon as she was standing erect, she knotted and swung her right fist in a rising arc. The blow she struck was delivered with a precision and force many a man might have envied. Certainly she had no cause for complaint over the effect it produced.

Driven with accuracy, by an obviously powerful body, the glove-encased hand took Eckland under the jaw. Beneath the thin sheath of leather, the knuckles had a hardness which went far beyond mere flesh and bone. Back snapped his head and, already close to toppling over, he went down like a steer struck by the pole-axe of a slaughterman at a hide and tallow factory.[1] When he landed, the back of his head smashed against the ground with some force. As he had been falling, a succession of brilliant lights had seemed to be erupting before his otherwise unseeing eyes. The impact brought the sensation to an end and, as he lay supine without any movement, everything went black for him.

Like the shotgun messenger, Walter Tract was taken completely unawares by the sudden change in the behavior of the woman they had stopped to help. What was more, he did not respond in a positive manner to the implied threat. However, the disincli-

1. A description of such a slaughterman in action can be found in: *THE HIDE AND TALLOW MEN*. J.T.E.

nation to react was not the result of a slow witted failure to appreciate the potential danger she was creating. Handling the ribbons of a Concord stagecoach was not work for a dullard and he was all too aware of what was in all probability portended by her actions. In spite of that, and his friendship with Eckland notwithstanding, he was forcing himself to think as the driver of the vehicle rather than a paid defender of it and its passengers, or a seeker after vengeance. As such, he was primarily concerned with ensuring he retained control over the six powerful horses and kept the reins in his grasp instead of releasing them with the intention of arming himself.

Even if the driver had felt inclined to take offensive action, a movement caught at the corner of his right eye drew his attention that way and warned he would have been doomed to failure!

Although they had avoided being located until the time was propitious, two masked and armed men were making an appearance by the right side of the trail. One came into view from behind a clump of bushes several feet away, holding a Winchester Model of 1873 carbine. Closer to the vehicle, grasping a Colt Civilian Model Peacemaker, the other was throwing aside a freshly cut clump of mesquite under which he had laid concealed until that moment. Nor were they all the support for the woman. A glance in the opposite direction informed Tract that another pair of outlaws had hidden in a similar fashion and were rising just as well equipped to deal with any attempted resistance on the part of those aboard the stagecoach.

Despite his passive response to the situation, Tract set about doing the only positive thing he could envisage. As he had no intention of trying to resist, he devoted himself to studying the male members of the gang. In spite of the multi-colored bandana each was using to conceal the majority of his features, the driver was seeking information which might serve to identify them. All were tallish, but not exceptionally so and their respective builds were no more than average for their height. Therefore, unless he could discover some more prominent indications to act as a guide, he realized that picking them out of a crowd would be very difficult.

The two men farthest away had on the everyday attire of cowhands, except that the garments showed no traces of the hard usage which invariably arose when working cattle. Having the appearance of being recently purchased, their hats were shaped in the style by which cowhands in Arizona sought to set themselves apart from those of other regions. Like the clothing, their gunbelts were such as could be bought ready-made in any town of reasonable size. The wooden handled Colt Peacemakers looked to be standard production models, as were the Winchester carbines they were lining at the stagecoach.

While that pair offered scant evidence to set them apart, Tract considered their companions might prove more fruitful. Going by various indications, they were of either pure or mixed Indian blood. Decorated by an eagle feather stuck under a dark blue band inscribed with medicine symbols, their black hats were high crowned in a fashion only rarely worn by white men in that day and age. From beneath the headdress, straight black hair hung to the level of the shoulders in each case, but the brims were drawn down sufficiently to aid the bandanas in preventing their features from being seen. However, the open necks of their fringed buckskin shirts displayed skin which was a dark brown in color as was their hands. Their brown trousers were tucked into the leggings of Navajo moccasions. On the left side of each gunbelt was a knife in a sheath which, like the hat bands, was of Indian manufacture.

"All right now!" yelled the man with the carbine on the left side of the trail, as he and his male companions started to converge upon the stagecoach. "Don't anybody try anything fancy happen you want to keep on living!"

"You do and you'll right soon regret it!" seconded the other outlaw armed with a Winchester, his voice also having a Mid-West accent. "We've got you covered from all sides and aren't bothered whether we take it from you alive or dead!"

"Wh—What the—?" began the unmistakable voice of Senator Paul Michael Twelfinch II from inside the vehicle.

"Do like they say, gents!" Tract advised. "They've

got us covered from both sides like he said and Ben—the shotgun messenger's down!"

As he was delivering the instructions, the driver hoped it would be obeyed. There had been a brittle timber to the voice of each outlaw. Despite the competence they had exhibited in preparing and carrying out the ambush, it suggested a nervousness which might erupt into violence if they believed things were going wrong. However, he was relieved by the thought that none of the passengers was likely to display hostile tendencies and he certainly had no intention of doing so.

"Now there's a right smart feller," the first outlaw declared. "Come on down here, but leave your gun behind. You fellers inside, wait until he's done it, then get out where we can take a look at you."

"Blue Buck!" called the woman, her accent that of a Southron. "You-all come on over and 'tend to this jasper."

Hearing her speak, Tract returned his gaze to the blonde. She was standing with her back to him and, going by her actions, was fastening a bandana so it would hide the bottom portion of her face. However, he was not allowed to give her a great deal of attention.

"You heard me, driver!" the first outlaw barked, coming across the trail in front of the horses as the man with the long black hair at the left side walked toward the woman. "Get down here, fast!"

Looping the ribbons around the handle of the

brake, Tract eased the Peacemaker from its holster using only the thumb and forefinger of the left hand. Placing it on the seat of the box, he climbed down. On reaching the ground and stepping away from the stagecoach, he saw the door open and the passengers began to emerge.

Middlesized and slim, the first man to leave the vehicle had a foppish appearance. There was a suggestion of Gallic origins about his swarthily handsome features which were emphasized by a small black chin beard and a moustache with its ends waxed to short points. Worn fussily and indicating he took considerable care over his appearance, his well cut clothing was in the height of current Eastern fashion. Although his movements were closer to mincing than might be regarded as desirable in most masculine company, they had a lithe and cat-like grace about them. It warned, if one took the trouble to study him, that there might be more to him than met the eye. He grasped a well polished black walking stick in his right hand, enfolding its silver knob daintily. However, strangely for that day, age and region, he gave no sign of carrying a firearm upon his person. Certainly he did not exhibit a gunbelt and holstered revolver.

"Toss away that fancy walking cane, *Monsieur* Jaqfaye of Paris, France!" ordered the outlaw acting as spokesman for the gang, pronouncing the honorific, "mon-sewer." "We wouldn't want no accidents with it."

"Whatever you wish, *m'sieur*," Pierre Henri Jaqfaye replied, his voice bearing a noticeable French accent and a timber less than masculine. "Although, if you have no objections, I would much prefer to lean it somewhere, so it will not become scratched or dirty."

"You just do that, happen you're so minded and just so long as you're real careful while you're doing it," the outlaw authorized. "But make good and goddamned sure you keep both hands in plain view all the while. Tommy Crane there might only be part Injun, but he could be all Injun way he's so suspicious natured."

"Ugh!" the second man with shoulder long black hair grunted gutterally, making a threatening gesture with his Colt. "That-um heap plenty true. Not trust-um paleface even if he look like fairy."

Directing a glare of bitter hatred at the speaker, Jaqfaye stepped quickly across to leave his cane against the front wheel of the stagecoach. Having done so, keeping his open hands in plain view although still showing his resentment over the derogatory comment, he turned and stood alongside the driver.

Slightly taller than the Frenchman and better built without being anywhere close to bulky, the next passenger was a few years younger. Brown haired and clean shaven, he wore spectacles which gave a studious look to his tanned and reasonably handsome face. Although he wore a black Stetson hat with a

Montana crown peak, the rest of his attire implied he
was a town dweller of moderate circumstances. He
too wore no visible armament and, on reaching the
ground, he went immediately to join Tract and Jaqfaye.

"Take it easy there, gents, I'm coming as fast as I
can," requested the third man to appear at the door
of the vehicle, his New England voice placatory.
"When you're *my* size, you can't move nowheres
near so spry as these slender fellers."

There was some justification for the assertion!

Having introduced himself as "Maurice Blenheim"
on boarding the stagecoach, and continuing to chat-
ter amiably throughout the journey, the speaker was
middle-sized and portly. Black haired, blue eyed and
perspiring freely, he had a cheerful face of the type to
inspire confidence in his honesty. He wore a white
"planter's" hat, shoved to the back of his head, a
matching two piece linen suit and shirt, with a multi-
colored silk cravat, and Hersome gaiter boots. As
was the case with his predecessors from the vehicle,
he showed no sign of being armed. Nor did he convey the impression of being any more of a fighting
man than the other two as, moving with a ponderous
slowness, he descended and walked to where they
were standing.

"Hey in there, it's your turn now!" called the
spokesman, after a few seconds had passed without
the last occupant leaving the stagecoach. "Haul your
god-damned butt outside here, *pronto*!"

"Do you know who you're talking to?" Twelfinch demanded, although his tone now was more querelous than pompous, peering out of the window.

"Sure I do, Senator," the spokesman admitted, showing no signs of being impressed or concerned by the knowledge. "And what I said still goes, only more so."

Muttering under his breath, Twelfinch rose and emerged with alacrity. Of slightly less than medium height and skinny, he was far from an impressive or commanding figure. Bareheaded, his white hair looked like a not too clean mop above a miserable face so thinly fleshed it resembled a skull. While costly, his Eastern style clothing hung loosely and untidily on his weedy body. That he should not show any indication of carrying weapons of any kind came as no surprise to anybody who knew him. He was an ardent and vociferous advocate of legislation to prevent ownership of firearms unless very stringent proof of need could be established.

"Hey, Belle!" the spokesman called, as the politician was going to stand alongside the rest of the passengers. "We've got—!"

"God damn it!" the blonde barked, turning to show she had fastened her blouse and concealed the lower half of her face beneath a folded bandana. Donning the hat she took from the man she had told to assist her, she went on just as heatedly as she strode forward leaving him to disarm the still motionless shotgun messenger. "Why don't you *tell* them who I am?"

"Sorry, B—!" the outlaw commenced.

"You damned nearly said it again!" the woman snorted, then ran her gaze along the line of men from the stagecoach. "All right, gents, let's start having you-all handing over your valuables. Being right respectful of important folks, Senator, we'll start with you-all."

"*Me?*" Twelfinch yelped and, taking a pace forward, looked by the next two passengers. "Jaqfaye, do *something*!"

"*Oui, M'sieur le* Senator," the Frenchman answered, his attitude indicating he was far from enamored of being singled out in such a fashion. "Tell me what you would have me *do* and I may *try,* but I do not hold out too much hope of whatever it is being successful."

"Damn it!" Twelfinch protested, being waved back to his place as he tried to go toward the man he was addressing. "Tell them who *you* are!"

"They appear to know all too well who I am, *m'sieur,*" Jaqfaye asserted mildly, but his voice took on a harder and more warning timber as he continued, "There's *nothing* I can tell them will make them change their minds. I would do as they tell you."

"B—But—But—!" the politician spluttered.

"Come on now, Senator, you being so all-fired eager to help the poor of the world and all," the spokesman interrupted, gesturing with the barrel of his Winchester. "You up and shell out afore we have Tommy Crane here do the asking."

"Ugh!" grunted the long haired outlaw, stepping forward and thrusting the muzzle of his Peacemaker in the direction of Twelfinch's stomach. "Hand-um over *wampum,* paleface law-maker, or maybe so me take-um your scalp."

"I—I—!" the politician gurgled, leaning forward to direct another look at Jaqfaye. Finding he was met with a stony indifference and clear disinclination to intercede on his behalf, he swung his eyes to the front and went on sulkily, "Very well, but you'll be sorry—!"

"Not half as god-damned sorry as you-all will be iffen you-all don't start to empty your pockets into Tommy Crane's hat!" the woman warned, in her heavily accented Southron tone. "Shell out fast, you 'mother-something' Yankee carpet-bagger. I'm getting quick out of patience!"

"Very well!" Twelfinch assented sullenly and with bad grace. As his right hand was reaching upward, it moved first toward the left breast of his jacket and hurriedly changed direction to disappear beneath the right side instead. Drawing out and offering a thin wallet, he muttered, "Here you are. Take it!"

"Now let's have it from the other side!" the blonde commanded, as the politician was dropping his property into the high crowned black hat proffered by the long haired outlaw.

"The *other* si—?" Twelfinch commenced.

"You're trying my patience again, god damn it!" the woman warned savagely. "Fetch out whatever it is you've got stashed away in there!"

"I—I—I—!" the politician babbled, once again glancing at the Frenchman. As he received not so much as a word in return, he gave a gesture of resignation and extracted a thick pocketbook bound in expensive red Morroco leather. "It's only this!"

"And very pretty it looks to me," the blonde claimed, reaching out to pluck the object from the reluctant grasp of its owner. Opening it, she glanced at the wad of high denomination bank notes it held and inquired sardonically, "What might these be, Senator, campaign funds?"

"N—!" Twelfinch began instinctively, then he nodded with vehemence. "Yes, that is what they are and when you hear who donated the—!"

"Senator!" Jaqfaye barked, his voice having lost its suggestion of lacking masculinity. "I would advise you not to try the patience of these people too far!"

"But I—!" Twelfinch gasped, glaring at the speaker as if unwilling to believe what he had heard.

"It is none of *my* affair, of course," the Frenchman put in. "But I consider you would be *most* ill-advised to say anything further, *m'sieur*!"

"I've never been one for listening to politicians jabbering either, Frenchie," the blonde supported, tossing the pocket-book into the hat. "My old daddy down home to Dixie always has a hankering for fancy do-hickeys like this, so I'll take it as a present for him."

"You can keep the money!" the politician offered. "But let me have the pocketbook back!"

"I told you what I aim to do with it," the woman replied.

"I'll buy it from you!" Twelfinch suggested, his bony hands reaching out.

"What with?" the blonde challenged. "Have you got some more money hidden away?"

"No!" the politician stated vehemently. "You've taken all I have on me, but I'll buy it back from you as soon as we reach Tucson."

"Why if that isn't the height of kindness," the woman said derisively. "Trouble being, even was we so inclined to go trusting you-all, we're not paying no visits to Tucson after we've done here."

"Damn it, Jaqfaye—!" Twelfinch almost shrieked.

"There's *nothing* I can do, or *say,* to help you!" the Frenchman declared, his bearing prohibitive. "Nor can I imagine why you would believe I might be able to do *anything* to influence these people."

"*You* for sure as hell couldn't," the woman affirmed and, ignoring Twelfinch as his mouth opened, she looked away from him to continue, "All right. Now it's your turn to give, fat man!"

"Whatever you say, young lady," Blenheim replied, his tone as amiable as it had been while chattering about inconsequential matters aboard the stagecoach. "Only I'm not a politician, so don't go expecting a wad of 'campaign funds' from me and you're welcome to what little I've got."

"Why isn't that just too kind of you-all?" the blonde purred, eyeing with obvious disdain the far from bulky wallet which the fat man had taken from the left inside breast pocket of his jacket. Taking and tossing it into the hat held by Tommy Crane, she went on, "And now we'll have the rest!"

"What *rest* would that be, ma'am?" Blenheim asked and he appeared to be genuinely puzzled as he posed the question.

"The *rest* that's in the money belt you've got on to make you look even fatter," the woman elaborated. "Come on now, you don't need to be bashful 'cause lil ole me's looking. You-all can just get to peeling it off and I promise not to peek."

"Well now, ma'am," Blenheim said, showing no greater indication of understanding, as he removed his hat with his left hand and mopped the back of the right across his brow. Then, reaching inside the crown as if to wipe the perspiration from the sweatband, he continued. "I don't know where you've got the—!"

"Kill him!" the woman yelled.

Instantly, the spokesman and Tommy Crane squeezed the triggers of their respective weapons. Both had been covering Blenheim from such a short range that a miss was almost impossible unless it was deliberately sought. Neither had tried to do so. Struck in the left side of the body by the two bullets, one .45 and the other .44 in caliber, the fat man was slammed backward against the stagecoach. Flying from his left hand, the planter's hat landed on the ground at the feet of the woman. Inside its crown, held by a spring clip, was a Remington Double Derringer.

"That lil ole stingy gun didn't do you any good at all, fat man," the blonde claimed, showing no sign of revulsion or remorse and paying no attention to what the other men from the stagecoach were doing. "Nor would that hide-out revolver behind your back you were planning to pull after you'd downed these two boys."

Chapter 3

THAT WAS BELLE STARR, GENTS

~~~~~

At the sound of the shots, the horses hitched to the stagecoach let out snorts of alarm. Instantly, acting upon his instinct as a driver, Walter Tract spun around and darted alongside them. By doing so, laudable though his behavior undoubtedly was, he was placing himself in jeopardy.

Instead of having joined the woman and his companions near the vehicle, the second outlaw armed with a Winchester Model of 1873 carbine was standing a short distance away from them. When he saw Tract begin to move, he let out a profane exclamation and started to turn the weapon in the same direction.

"Easy there!" the youngest passenger advised, speaking in a firm yet gentle New England voice as he stepped forward quickly. Halting between the muzzle of the carbine and the target at which it was being pointed, he spread his hands, palms forward, outward from his sides as an indication of pacific intentions. His tone remained cool, calm and steady as he continued, "The driver's only going to stop the team bolting."

For a moment, Jedroe Franks thought he had saved Tract at the cost of his own life!

Above the masking bandana, the eyes of the outlaw flared with a mixture of alarm and panic!

Looking down, Franks watched the knuckle of the right forefinger becoming white as it tightened on the trigger!

Regardless of his studious appearance, the slender young passenger knew enough about firearms to appreciate the full extent of the danger!

If the pressure continued to be exerted, the point would be reached when the sear was disengaged!

Then the hammer would be liberated to snap forward and detonate the charge in the waiting cartridge!

Even as the far from pleasant thought was formulating, Franks noticed something which came as a mixture of relief and surprise. Instead of being at the fully cocked position, the hammer was forward. Clearly, unlike his companion who was armed in a similar fashion, the outlaw had failed to take the precaution of operating the loading lever to feed a bullet from the tubular magazine to the chamber of the barrel. Until this was done, the weapon would not fire.

However, having made a study of human nature, the relief which Franks started to experience was quickly tempered by a far less reassuring thought!

When the outlaw discovered the mistake he had made, he seemed sufficiently nervous to rectify it!

Should this happen, although Franks was taking care not to offer any cause, the weapon might be fired as soon as the reloading was completed!

Regardless of the summations he was drawing, the young passenger did not attempt to bring out the Colt Storekeeper Model Peacemaker revolver from its "half breed" spring retention shoulder holster beneath the left side of his jacket. While he had not been questioned about, or deprived of the weapon, what had happened to Maurice Blenheim warned him that its presence might be known to the gang. Even if this was not the case, despite carrying it for self defense, he knew he lacked the skill of a trained gun fighter. He could shoot with reasonable accuracy, but did not possess the kind of speed in handling it which alone might save him from being shot by the outlaw covering him. Furthermore, even should he have had the requisite ability, he was aware it would only prolong his life momentarily. As soon as he gave such an unmistakable indication that he was armed, the other male members of the gang would open fire upon him. No matter how quickly he moved, he would not be able to render them all *hors de combat* swiftly enough to prevent himself being shot.

Another consideration served to cause Franks to stand immobile. Although the killing of Blenheim had not done so, any further gun play might provoke the outlaws into shooting at everybody who had been aboard the stagecoach. While he had no sympathy with the philosophies advocated by Senator Paul Michael Twelfinch II, he had no desire to be responsible for the deaths of the politician, Pierre Henri Jaqfaye, the driver and the unconscious shotgun messenger.

The matter was taken out of Franks' hands!

"Max!" the woman snapped, having looked around when Tract and the young passenger moved, before any decision need be taken by the latter.

"Yes?" asked the outlaw, glancing over his shoulder and, while doing so, swinging the barrel of the Winchester out of its alignment on the chest of the young man.

"Send him to help the driver hold the horses," the blonde commanded. "It wouldn't be good old Southern hospitality for us'n's to have these gentlemen left a-foot because the stagecoach ran away on them, now would it?"

"I reckon you're right at that, Sa—*Belle*," the outlaw conceded, allowing his right forefinger to relax an instant before it had reached the critical point. Returning his attention to Franks, he went on in a harder and more demanding tone, "You heard Miss Sta—*the lady*. Go and do what she said!"

"That was what I intending to do," Franks claimed, trying with some success to prevent the brittle tension he was experiencing from tinging his voice. "But I didn't want to get shot before I started."

"Smart feller, for a city-bred dude," the blonde declared. "Mind you keep an eye on them while they're doing it, Max."

"Sure!" the outlaw replied shortly, his demeanor suggesting he resented being reminded to take such a basic precaution.

"Give me the hat, Tommy Crane," the woman ordered, swinging her gaze back to the pair standing over the body. "Then get the fat man's money belt!"

"M—!" the long haired outlaw croaked, losing the deep and guttural tone. *"Me?"*

"Yes, *you*!" snapped the blonde, snatching the hat she had requested from its owner. "And don't take all god-damned day doing it, you 'mother-something' *half-breed*!"

Attracted by what was being said, Franks threw a glance over his shoulder as he was walking to where Tract was holding the heads of the lead team. He discovered that Crane was looking at the other outlaw who shared responsibility for the death of the fat man. However, on the woman delivering her second comment, the long haired bandit glared in her direction for a moment. Then, with obvious reluctance, he returned the Colt to its holster and bent over the corpse.

Arriving by the driver, Franks found there was no

need for his services. Aided by the dead weight of the coach standing with its brakes applied, Tract had had no difficulty in keeping the horses under control. Satisfied on that point, the young man watched what was happening elsewhere. He found that Twelfinch was taking advantage of the gang's attention being diverted.

On striking the side of the stagecoach under the impulsion of the two heavy caliber bullets, Blenheim had rebounded and fallen a few feet away. Seeing the woman and male outlaws were not paying attention to him, the politician had shuffled sideways until he was standing alongside Jaqfaye.

"Why—?" Twelfinch began, only just retaining sufficient presence of mind to hold down his voice to slightly louder than a whisper.

"Not *now,* damn you!" the Frenchman hissed back. "This isn't the time, or the place, to try to get back your money *that* way!"

"But if they knew who you're wor—!" the politician commenced.

"They could be so worried they killed us both!" Jaqfaye warned, selecting an argument which he considered would be likely to produce the result he required. Seeing the alarm which came to the skull-like features of the other passenger, he went on, "Don't worry, *M'sieur le* Senator, I promise that you won't be the loser. If the worst comes to the worst, I personally will reimburse you for all they have taken."

"Want to thank you for what you did just now,

young feller, that son-of-a-bitch was figuring to put a blue window in me," Tract remarked. "Doing what you did took nerve, but some'd say you didn't show real good sense in doing it."

"I'd acted before I had time to think about the consequences," Franks admitted, wishing he could hear what was being said between the politician and the Frenchman.

"You done good, no matter why," the driver praised. "There's some young 'n's's would've hoisted out that hid-away gun you're toting and started to make smoke regardless. Which, with yahoos as jumpy as that bunch look to be, would've gotten more than just *you* made wolf-bait happen you know what that means."

"I know what it means," Franks admitted, pleased with the confirmation of his assessment where the outlaws were concerned until another thought struck him. "You *know* I'm armed?"

"Ben told me you was," Tract explained. "He's better'n fair at seeing guns's folks think're hid away out of sight and sneaky-like, although he never mentioned that Blenheim feller was toting." Looking to where the shotgun messenger was just starting to stir, watched dispassionately by the second long haired outlaw, he went on with a mixture of anger and grudging admiration, "God damn it though, young feller, that gal must pack a punch like a son-of-a-bitching knobhead mule kicking way he went down when she hit him."

"I'd say, from the way he dropped, she has a set of brass knuckles under the gauntlet," Franks assessed. "Good as she swung, I doubt whether her hand alone would be hard enough to do it. From what I learned while boxing at college, the way she hit his jaw, she would have broken her knuckles without some form of protection for them."

"I'll float my stick along of you on that," the driver conceded, deciding there was more to the young passenger than met the eye. "Do you know who she is?"

"No."

"She's—!"

"Hey, you pair!" the woman called, before Tract could deliver the information. "Now you have the horses calmed down, let's be having you-all back here."

"You heard the lady!" growled the outlaw who was keeping watch over the driver and the young passenger. "Get moving!"

"How's about letting me go take care of Ben there?" Tract suggested, jerking his right thumb in the direction of the shotgun messenger.

"You can do what the hell you like with him after we've finished with you and pulled out," the outlaw with the Winchester replied and gestured with the weapon. "But, right now, do what you're told."

"All right, Frenchie," the woman said, as the driver and Franks joined the surviving pair of passengers. "You-all can shell out now."

"As you wish, *mademoiselle*," Jaqfaye replied, reaching almost daintily into the left side of his jacket. "Or is it *'madame'*?"

"Last time good ole Calamity Jane was asked that," the blonde answered, "she said, 'I'm not a madam, I'm just one of the gals.'"

"Would that have been after she beat you in that fight in Butte, Montana, ma'am?" Franks inquired, with what appeared to be an innocent and respectful eagerness.

"You've got real sharp ears, smart-ass," the woman stated. "But you-all have gotten it all wrong. It was m—*Belle Starr* who gave Calamity Jane the licking."

"That would have been the time in *Butte,* Montana, ma'am?" the youngest passenger asked in the same interested fashion.

"Where else would it have been, smart-ass, w—*they* only locked horns the one time," the woman replied, then turned her attention back to Jaqfaye. "All right, Frenchie, put it up for lil ole me."

"Of course, *mademoiselle*," the Frenchman assented, his manner nonchalant. "Here you are."

"You-all are coming across way too easy, Frenchie," the blonde claimed. "Give me your carbine and check him out, Max. I reckon he'd sooner have you do it than me."

"Do you think he's got one of those money belts on?" inquired the man who had kept watch on Franks and Tract, surrendering the Winchester.

"Find out," the blonde commanded, glancing at the weapon she accepted and, giving a hiss of annoyance, working its lever to charge the chamber.

Having kept the Frenchman under observation, Franks could see he deeply resented the implication of being a homosexual and was struggling to keep control of his temper. As Max stepped toward him, he darted a glance to where his walking stick was leaning against the front wheel of the stagecoach. For a moment, he reminded the youngest passenger of a cat preparing to spring. Then, giving a particularly Gallic shrug of resignation, he spread open his arms.

"Nothing!" Max announced disgustedly, at the conclusion of the search.

"Nothing?" the woman repeated.

"I have an establishment in Tucson, as well as at Phoenix, so keep bank accounts in each place," Jaqfaye explained, lowering his arms. "Therefore, I do not need to carry large sums when travelling from one to the other."

"Looks like we'll have to make do with what we've got from you in that case," the woman answered. "Now it's your turn, smart-ass."

"I'm like *M'sieur* Jaqfaye, ma'am, only poorer," Franks asserted, extracting his wallet with his left hand. "All I have is here."

"This isn't much for a smart-ass young feller who's travelling, only *you* won't have bank accounts scattered around," the woman said pensively, watching the young man while Max tipped the contents into the hat held by Tommy Crane and tossed the wallet on to the ground. "Anyways, I'm not from Missouri, but I still have to be shown. Give him a going over."

"He's toting a *gun*!" Max yelped, on commencing the task, jerking free the Colt Storekeeper Model Peacemaker.

"He's not breaking any laws by carrying one," the blonde replied disdainfully and showing no concern over what might have proven a costly omission in failing to have the passengers searched. "How about more money?"

"None I can find," Max admitted a few seconds later, having tossed aside the short barelled revolver and run his hands over the clothing of its owner.

"Now that's strange!" the woman purred, looking straight at Franks' face as she had ever since ordering the search. "I've still got this feeling that he's carrying more than we've laid hands on."

"All right," Max said. "Let me stick the carbine under his chin and give him a count of five to tell us where it is."

"And what will you do if he keeps quiet, shoot him?"

"Yes."

"Then how the 'something' will he tell us?" the woman snorted. Stepping closer, she placed the muzzle of the carbine under Jaqfaye's chin and went on, "I'm counting to five, smart-ass, then I'll spread his brains all over the range I'm so sure you've got more money hid away. If that doesn't work, I'll do the same with the driver. One! Two!"

Looking at the Frenchman, Franks was impressed by the way in which he was behaving. If he was lacking in masculinity, it certainty did not extend to physical courage. It was not, the young man felt sure, fear which caused him to stand like a statue. His face was impassive and only a slight tightening of the lips showed he appreciated his deadly peril. It implied he did not doubt the threat would be carried out. For all that, he made no attempt to speak, whether to ask for mercy or suggest a surrender to the demand.

"Three! Four!"

"All right, you win!" Franks acceded, his belief being strengthened that there was more to the Frenchman than met the eye. "It's in my carpetbag in the front boot."

"Take him to fetch it, Max!" the woman ordered, stepping away from Jaqfaye. "Haven't you finished, Tommy Crane?"

"Yes I have!" the long haired outlaw affirmed, displaying the money belt he was holding between the tips of his right fingers and thumb.

In the earlier stages of the conversation between the blonde and the passengers, Franks had contrived to keep Tommy Crane under observation. It had become increasingly apparent that he found the task to which he was assigned most distasteful. He had handled the corpse hesitantly and with care, clearly being disinclined to touch it. On having removed the money belt from beneath the shirt of the dead man, finding his hands had become stained by blood, he had shown what was obviously revulsion and, going to the edge of the trail hurriedly, wiped them clean on the grass. Stepping back as soon as he had handed over the belt, he rubbed his palms vigorously against the legs of his trousers and gave a sigh of relief.

"Hey!" ejaculated the outlaw who had acted as spokesman, gazing across the range. "Where the hell as Fio—*Fred* got to? S—He should be coming by now."

"Here *he* is," the woman replied, laying great emphasis upon the second word, as she turned to look in the same direction. "All right, Tommy Crane, get up on the box and empty the guns."

Having been compelled to divert his attention from the long haired outlaw by the need to unload his carpetbag from the luggage boot beneath the driver's box, Franks found the comments sufficiently intriguing to decide he would see what had caused them. He discovered that a rider leading four saddled horses was coming from one of the clumps of woodland which, unbeknown to him, had been studied with misgivings by Benjamin Eckland prior to the hold up.

Shorter than the woman and the male outlaws, the newcomer appeared to be very stocky in build. This, Franks concluded, could be due as much to clothing as physical characteristics. A low crowned black Stetson was pulled down sufficiently to hide the hair inside it and a bandana covered almost all of the face.

Worn despite the heat, with the exception of black gloves and Levi's trousers tucked into smallish brown riding boots, a voluminous yellow "fish" slicker concealed whatever lay beneath it.

"Where the hell have you been?" the spokesman yelled angrily, as the newcomer brought the horses to a halt some thirty yards away.

"It's not that important, blast you!" the woman stated, before any reply could be made. "Have you-all unloaded those guns yet, Tommy Crane?"

"Not yet!" the long haired outlaw answered with asperity, from the box of the stagecoach. Tipping the shells from the twin barrels of the shotgun he had broken open, he continued with no trace of his earlier guttural accent, "I've only got one pair of hands, you know."

"Then use them instead of talking, you stupid *half-breed* son-of-a-bitch!" the blonde ordered and returned her attention to the victims of the hold up. "If you know what's good for you, you-all won't try loading those guns until we're well out of sight. Just let us see any of you-all so much as look like that's what you're figuring on doing and we'll come back to give you-all exactly the same as that fat jasper there got."

"Here it is!" Max announced, waving the bulky carpetbag he had been given by the young passenger. "I'll get—!"

"Fetch the god-damned thing with us!" the woman interrupted. "We've wasted too much time already."

Backing away as she was speaking, followed by the spokesman and Max, the woman made for the horses. Dropping the shotgun and snatching up the Colt Peacemaker discarded by the driver, Tommy Crane tucked it into his waistband. Then, clambering down with haste, he scuttled rather than merely hurried after them. While this was happening, the second long haired outlaw looked to where Eckland was struggling dazedly into a sitting position. Swinging the right hand revolver he had unloaded, he laid the barrel with savage force against the side of its owner's head. As the shotgun messenger subsided once more, he gave a laugh and, tossing down both Colts, strode rapidly to join the rest of the party.

"Don't try it!" Franks advised urgently, his anger at losing the carpetbag containing all his savings and other items of property he prized highly being swamped by hearing Tract rip out a profanity on seeing what happened to Eckland and make as if to go after the assailant.

"You're likely right, young feller!" the driver admitted bitterly, after a moment during which he appeared on the point of disregarding the counsel. "But I surely hope I meet the half-breed son-of-a-bitch some time when I'm packing iron. Trouble being, it's not likely I'll get the chance." He swung his gaze from Eckland to each living passenger in turn and went on in tones of certainty, "That was Belle Starr, gents. Which being, she'll have their get-away planned so god-damned well they'll all be to hell and gone clear long afore we can set the law on their trail."

"Then let's get going without any more delay!" Twelfinch demanded.

"We'll light out just's soon's it's safe to do it, Senator," Tract promised, his voice cold, watching the gang riding away at a fast trot. "And after I've 'tended to Ben there. While I'm doing it, you gents can be getting Mr. Blenheim loaded."

"*Loaded?*" the politician repeated, looking with a mixture of revulsion and alarm at the body. "You mean loaded *inside* with m—us?"

"No!" Tract denied, making no attempt to conceal his annoyance and impatience. His tone became coldly challenging as he continued, "On the goddamned roof. But Ben'll be riding inside—Happen *you* don't have no objections, *Senator*?"

"I—I don't!" Twelfinch asserted, refusing to meet the savage gaze of the driver and suspecting any other decision would not be supported by Jaqfaye or the young man.

"I'll wrap the body in a tarp while you're attending to the guard, Mr. Tract, if you have one," Franks offered, although he had appeared to be on the point of making a comment when the driver mentioned the well known woman outlaw, Belle Starr. But he had refrained and devoted himself to watching the gang taking their departure. "Then, if these gentlemen will lend a hand, I'll put it on the roof."

"I will assist you, *m'sieur*," Jaqfaye offered, but the politician did not duplicate the sentiment.

Instead, throwing a querilous glance across the range, Twelfinch inquired, "I—Is it s—safe for you to start moving about?"

"Safe enough, I reckon," the driver assessed, looking in the same direction. "By the time you're getting the body on top, those son-of-bitches will be out of sight. But, to make sure, we'll wait until they are afore we do anything."

"I agree with you, *m'sieur*," the Frenchman said firmly.

"And me," Franks supported.

"And you, my young friend," Jaqfaye went on. "I am greatly in your debt. There are many who would have allowed me to be killed."

"I suppose so," Franks admitted, non-committally.

"Do not worry about your losses," the Frenchman said reassuringly. "I will personally refund all they took."

"That's very good of you and I'm obliged," Franks replied, his gratitude genuine. "But, damn it, I hate being robbed."

"So do I," Jaqfaye seconded, his voice very quiet yet—to the youngest passenger at least—somehow as menacing as if he had screamed imprecations. "But, it is preferable to resisting, as *M'sieur* Blenheim proved. There is always another day."

"Let's hope it isn't long coming!" Franks said,

thinking he would not care to be any of the outlaws who fell into the hands of the outwardly effeminate Frenchman. "Can we make a st—?"

"Oh my god!" Twelfinch yelped, pointing, before the question could be completed. "Look there. Are they more robbers?"

Chapter 4

GO AFTER THE GANG

~~~

ATTRACTED BY THE ALARM IN THE VOICE OF THE politician, Walter Tract, Jedroe Franks and Pierre Henri Jaqfaye did as he had requested!

Two riders, one leading a big paint stallion, were coming slowly around the bend of the trail from which the driver and Benjamin Eckland had received their first sight of the woman!

Although he did not answer what he considered to have been a most tactless question from Senator Paul Michael Twelfinch II, Tract was well versed in the ways of the West and he started to draw conclusions based upon what he could see.

From the shape of each rider's low crowned and wide brimmed J.B. Stetson hat and other signs, the driver assumed they were Texans. They wore the attire of working cowhands and showed signs of hard travelling. However, despite the fact that the man leading the paint was seated on the horse used to aid the deception by the woman, he did not believe they intended any mischief. On the other hand, while they exchanged glances and brief comments at the sight ahead of them, they did not increase the pace at which they were moving.

Sitting the poor quality horse with easy grace, the taller of the pair being in his late 'teens, was also the younger. Wide shouldered and lean of waist, he was blond haired, clean shaven and handsome. Tightly rolled and knotted about his throat, a scarlet bandana trailed its long ends down the front of his dark blue shirt and brown and white calfskin vest. Turned back into two inches wide cuffs, the legs of his faded Levi's trousers hung outside high heeled and sharp toed riding boots with Kelly Petmaker spurs on their heels. Around his waist was an exceptionally well designed brown *buscadero* gunbelt carrying a brace of staghorn handled Colt Artillery Peacemakers in holsters capable of allowing them to be drawn with great speed provided the wearer possessed the requisite skill to utilize the quality.

Tract assessed that the blond had the necessary ability!

As well as lacking some two inches of his companion's height, at around six foot, the second rider was also more slender in build. Like Franks, his features suggested a studious mien. However, while they were pallid, this was because his skin resisted tanning rather than because he led a sedentary and indoor life. His hair was black and a neatly trimmed moustache graced his top lip. With one exception, he was dressed in the same manner as the blond. Instead of wearing a vest, he had on a brown jacket. Its right side was stitched back to offer unimpeded access to the solitary ivory butted Colt Civilian Model Peacemaker in the holster of a black gunbelt of an equally competent manufacture.

In the summation of the driver, here again was a capable gun handler!

Having completed his study of the newcomers and drawn his conclusions about them, Tract gave his attention to the horses. The paint led by the blond and the equally large black stallion his companion was sitting were magnificent animals. Despite showing indications of having been ridden hard for some time, neither could be controlled by a man unskilled in matters equestrian. Although the former was favoring its right fore leg in a way which suggested why the youngster was using the much poorer specimen, Tract decided it had only thrown a shoe and was not suffering from an injury. Both saddles were low of horn and—as Texans said, instead of "cinch" had—double girths, after the fashion evolved in the Lone Star State. Each had a coiled lariat fastened to the horn, a tarpaulin wrapped bedroll strapped to the cantle and a Winchester rifle, butt pointing to the rear for easy withdrawal on dismounting, attached to the left side. On the opposite side to his lariat, the slimmer rider carried a black leather bag of the kind in which doctors kept the tools of their profession when travelling.

"Howdy, you-all," greeted the blond, bringing the horses to a halt. He pronounced the words, "Heidi, yawl" in a fashion which announced he had been born and raised in Texas. He continued, "Looks like you've had more than a mite of trouble, gents."

"There's some as might just up and say 'yes' to that," Tract replied, reading the brand on the paint as "CA" and knowing the ranch in the Lone Star State which used such a sign to identify its livestock.

If the blond rode for the CA ranch, the driver concluded, the chances were greatly in favor of him being better than average when it came to handling a gun!

"The gang who robbed us rode off that way!" Twelfinch put in, gesturing in the rough direction of where the outlaws had already disappeared amongst the trees. "Get after them!"

"How?" the blond inquired, turning a far from respectful gaze to the politician. "This ole Dusty horse of mine threw him a shoe back a ways and I'm surely not fixing on going chasing a bunch of owlhoots on this no-account crowbait we come across straying back there."

"Then *you* go after the—!" Twelfinch commanded, cheeks reddening with anger at the rebuff, swinging his eyes to the other newcomer.

"Are both of them cashed in, friend?" the second

cowhand inquired, his accent just as indicative of "roots" in Texas, addressing the driver and giving the politician not so much as a glance.

"Only that gent," Tract answered, indicating the body of Maurice Blenheim with a wave of his right hand. "But I haven't gotten around yet to finding out how bad hurt Ben there is."

"Which being," the slender Texan declared, starting to swing from his saddle. "I'd best take a look."

"*You?*" the politician asked disdainfully, the annoyance he felt at the way he had been ignored combining with his radical antipathy toward Southrons in general and provoking the question when his other instincts warned it might prove ill-advised.

"Are any of you gents for-real and regular doctors?" the blond drawled, when his companion did not deign to reply, making it obvious he was not including Twelfinch in the query.

"I'm not," Franks replied, responding to the interrogative glance directed his way by the driver.

"Neither am I, I'm afraid," Jaqfaye seconded, although he did not receive a similar hint from Tract.

"Which being," the blond Texan stated. "I'd stand well clear, was I you-all, and let Doc go to it."

"*Doc?*" the driver queried hopefully, gazing first at the wedge-shaped brand on the flank of the big black stallion. Then he lifted his eyes to take in the pallid features of the man who had ridden it and went on, "Don't like to sound nosy, friend, but would you be Doc Leroy?"

"The name's Marvin Eldridge Leroy," the slender cowhand informed, unstrapping the black bag from his saddlehorn. "But I've been called 'Doc' on occasion."

"And worse, more than just on occasion and always deserved," the blond asserted, looking at Tract. "My name's 'Waco,' *amigo*. Is there anything I can be doing while Doc's 'tending to that feller, him getting riled real easy 'n' sudden should folk get underfoot when he's doctoring."

"You could take his horse and go after the gang!" Twelfinch suggested, in a tone which implied he expected to be obeyed.

"Well now, I *could* just do that," the younger Texan conceded, his voice almost caressingly mild, as he was dismounting. "Only, seeing's how ole Snowy there's been toting Doc and me both for a fair spell afore we come across this miserable crowbait I've been forking, I sure as hell don't aim to push him no more by doing it."

"But, god damn it, man, they robbed m—*us*!" the politician protested in righteous indignation.

"Go after them yourself, happen you feel so strong about it, I'll loan you a gun," Waco answered and, with the manner of one who considered the subject under discussion was at an end, turned to the driver. "I'll give you a hand to get that dead *hombre* loaded on the coach, was such your intention, *amigo*."

"Be obliged if you wo—!" Tract commenced.

"How's about thinking about the feller who's alive

afore you bother over the one who's already cashed in?" Doc Leroy interrupted. "What happened to him?"

"The gal who was running the whole she-bang knocked him down, wearing a knuckle-duster likely, first off," Tract supplied, seeing the wisdom behind the question. "Then one of her men pistol whipped him when he showed signs of coming 'round."

"Sound like real neighborly folks," Waco commented. "Can us common fellers get to doing it now, *sir?*"

"Feel free," Doc assented, the question having been addressed to him.

"Hey, though!" Tract ejaculated, looking at the blond with renewed interest. "Aren't you the 'Waco' who rides with Cap'n Fog and the OD Connected's floating outfit?"

"There's only the one's I know of," the younger Texan declared with a grin.

"Which same's *four* too god-damned many, most times," Doc called over his shoulder, as he set off toward the motionless shotgun messenger with purposeful and confident strides. "You keep him hard to work, mind, friend. He gets fractious when he's let stand idle."

"Sounds like he knows you real well, young feller," the driver remarked amiably, satisfied his friend was in capable hands. "Would Cap'n Fog, Mark Counter 'n' the Ysabel Kid be around?"

"Not happen our luck holds good," Waco replied,

but there was a wistful note in his drawl as he thought of the three men—Captain Dustine Edward Marsden "Dusty" Fog, C.S.A., in particular—who he regarded, along with his present companion, as being closer than brothers.[1] "I took lead in a shooting fuss over to Backsight and had to stay on for a spell,[2] but Doc and me're headed back home to Rio Hondo County, Texas, as soon as we've finished the chore we're 'tending to."

Which proved that, competent as he undoubtedly was in several other fields of endeavor, the blond youngster rated pretty low as a prophet.[3]

While the other men were talking, satisfied there was nothing to fear from the newcomers, Franks had gone to and opened the baggage boot at the rear of the stagecoach. There was a trunk and three large wicker baskets inscribed, "JAQFAYE OF PARIS" inside, but he had no difficulty in locating the items he was seeking. Removing the roll of tarpaulin and rope, he carried them to the body where he was joined by Waco and Tract. Remembering the offer of assistance made by the Frenchman, he expected it would be forgotten now other help was available. However, seeing

---

1. Information regarding the careers and special qualifications of Captain Dustine Edward Marsden "Dusty" Fog, C.S.A., Mark Counter and the Ysabel Kid, can be found in various volumes of the *Civil War* and *Floating Outfit* series. J .I.E.

2. How the wound came about is described in: *RETURN TO BACKSIGHT*. J.T.E.

3. Details of the background and special qualifications of Waco are recorded in: *Appendix One*. Why his judgment was at fault is told in the *Waco* series. J.T.E.

the politician was making for him, giving a gesture of obvious prohibition and rejection, Jaqfaye walked across to ask what he could do to help.

Going quickly to where Eckland was lying, all the levity Doc had employed when speaking to Waco left him and he became oblivious of everything else around him. His instincts warned that he had a difficult task ahead of him, but he did not allow the thought to distress or disturb him.

Although he had not yet been able to attain his ambition of becoming a qualified doctor, as his late father was who had encouraged him to do so, the slender young man who—apart from his pallid face—looked like a typical cowhand of Texas was already very knowledgeable in medical matters. Ever since the murder of his parents in a budding range war had caused him to put aside his departure to medical school in St. Louis,[4] he had taken every opportunity to study and improve his practical skills. What was more, while earning his living first as a hand with the Wedge trail crew delivering herds of cattle on contract for small ranchers,[5] then as a member of General Jackson Baines "Ole Devil" Hardin's

---

4. The reason for the range war in which the parents of Marvin Eldridge "Doc" Leroy were murdered and how he finally achieved his ambition to qualify as a doctor is told in: *DOC LEROY, M.D.* J.T.E.

5. The whole of the Wedge contract trail drive crew make "guest" appearances in: *QUIET TOWN, TRIGGER FAST* and *GUN WIZARD*. However, Marvin Eldridge "Doc" Leroy alone takes an active part in the events recorded in: *SET A-FOOT*. How he and Waco teamed up and he decided to join the floating outfit of the OD Connected ranch is told in: *Part Five, "The Hired Butcher," THE HARD RIDERS.* J.T.E.

legendary floating outfit,[6] he had found numerous opportunities to engage upon the profession to which he aspired. In fact, due to the number with which he had been called upon to deal, he could even now claim to know more about the treatment of gunshot wounds than many a practitioner who had earned the honorific, "Doctor of Medicine." In addition to these and other injuries which came the way of cowhands, he had on occasion found the need to deliver babies and, in the not too distant future, would be compelled to cope with the problem of bringing recalcitrant twins into the world.[7]

All in all, therefore, Marvin Eldridge "Doc" Leroy had no reason to doubt his ability to handle whatever might lay ahead!

Setting down his medical bag so it would be readily available to his hands, the slender Texan knelt to commence his examination of the unmoving shotgun messenger. Even if he had not received the information from Tract, he could have guessed at least something of what had taken place to cause the condition to which Eckland was reduced. From previous experiences, when celebrating cowhands had been pistol whipped by the "fighting pimp" peace officers infest-

---

6. Information regarding the career and special qualifications of General Jackson Baines "Ole Devil" Hardin, C.S.A., are to be found in the *Ole Devil Hardin* series, *Part Four, "Mr. Colt's Revolving Cylinder Pistol," J.T.'S HUNDREDTH*—which cover his early life—various volumes of the *Civil War* and *Floating Outfit* series and his death is reported in: *DOC LEROY, M.D.* J.T.E.

7. Told in: *Chapter Two, "The Juggler And The Lady," WACO RIDES IN.* J.T.E.

ing some of the Kansas trail end towns, the sight of the swollen and discolored ridge showing through the hair—the guard having lost his hat when the woman knocked him down—where the barrel of the Peacemaker had struck the side of the head was sufficient to establish how it was created.

The first task, Doc realized, was to ascertain just how seriously his patient was injured. He knew the condition referred to as "unconsciousness," or "insensibility," was due to interruption of the action of the brain through some form of interference with the functioning of the body's nervous system. Apart from ordinary sleep, there were two degrees of unconsciousness; partial, or "stupor" and the vastly more serious complete insensibility known as "coma."

Although there was an excessive flow of saliva tinged with blood oozing out of the mouth of the shotgun messenger, suggesting the driver was correct regarding the way in which the woman had protected her fist against damage prior to striking him, Doc wanted to establish the exact nature of his unconscious state before conducting any physical tests on the jaw. First, the Texan tried speaking to Eckland. Providing the stupor was not too great, the sufferer could sometimes be aroused by the sound of a voice. There was no sign of it happening on this occasion. Reaching with both hands, the Texan next took hold of the lashes of the right eye and pulled them gently in opposite directions.

"Damn it!" Doc breathed, when there was no resistance to his actions and the eyelids separated instead of contracting; as would have happened in the case of even a heavy stupor. What was more, despite suddenly being subjected to the bright light of the sun—which should have caused the muscular ring known as the "iris" to shrink and the size of the pupil to diminish—they remained immobile. "It's a deep coma for sure, likely with a fracture to the skull."

Releasing the eyelids, Doc glanced to satisfy himself that the teeth of the guard were natural. If they had been false, they would have needed to be taken out before he did anything else. Then, as the breathing remained quiet, he removed and folded his jacket to make an extemporized pillow. Raising the head and shoulders slightly, with it as a support, he turned the former so the injured side was uppermost. As he did so, he was ready to modify the position if the breathing became in any way difficult or obstructed.

Moving his seemingly boneless hands with great care, the Texan ran the tip of the right forefinger along the contused ridge. With a sensation of relief, he found no irregularity and concluded there was a chance his fear of a fracture might be misplaced. Gambling upon this proving the case, he gave his attention to the jaw. In addition to being badly swollen and bruised where the punch had landed, his gently questing fingers felt the crepitus caused by the broken section of the bone grating against one another. The extreme depth of the coma was further indicated by the complete lack of response from Eckland to the treatment. However, an examination of the mouth proved the tongue was not cut. Nor was the extent of the damage so severe, as might have happened if the injury was caused by a bullet, that it was liable to slip back and impede breathing.

For all the positive results acquired by his scrutiny, Doc did not for a moment consider he was faced with a sinecure!

The Texan was engaged in the kind of a situation where, lacking the aids to diagnosis which would be available to a later generation, a doctor in the late 1870s—particularly on the great range country west of the Mississippi River—had to rely upon his knowledge, judgment and instincts!

While he had not qualified, Doc had to reach a decision regarding treatment upon which the life of another human being could depend!

If he was correct about the extent of the damage caused by the barrel of the pistol, Doc could bandage the broken jaw. To do so, should the skull be fractured, would apply a pressure and compression to the former injury, no matter how carefully he applied the bandages, which could prove fatal. On the other hand, if left unsecured, the journey to the nearest town would offer opportunities for further damage to the jaw which could prove just as fatal as an incorrect summation regarding the condition of the skull.

A lesser man might have called upon Tract, as Eckland's friend, Waco, or the passengers of the stagecoach, for an opinion!

That was not the way in which the late Eldridge Jason Leroy, M.D., had taught his son to behave!

The decision was for Doc and Doc alone to take!

"Damn it, Sir John, why couldn't you have been a storekeeper instead of a doctor?" the slender Texan mused wryly, employing the sobriquet by which his father had been known to differentiate between himself, "Lil Doc." Opening the black bag, he lifted out a roll of wide white bandage and went on, "Life would surely be more easy for me if you had!"

Chapter 5

THAT MAN TRIED TO KILL ME

~~~

"I'VE COME UP ON YOU AT LAST, YOU MURDERING son-of-a-bitch!"

Hearing the words as he was dismounting from his big and, at present, hard ridden bay gelding at four-thirty in the afternoon, Major Bertram Mosehan looked around. What he saw gave warning that, even if such provocative words were ever intended to be part of rough cowhand horseplay, their current intent was in deadly earnest. For all that, he was at a loss to decide why they were being directed his way.

Considering to whom it was being uttered, there were many people in Arizona Territory and elsewhere throughout the United States of America who would have thought the words extremely ill-advised!

Tall, wide shouldered, in his early forties, Mosehan bore himself with the straight backed posture of a professional soldier. Moderately handsome, sun bronzed, his mouth was firm and shielded by a close clipped brown moustache. A touch of gray at his temples gave a maturity to a strong countenance which indicated he was not a man with whom it would be safe to trifle. He had on a tan Stetson with a "Montana crown" peak, a waist length brown leather jacket, dark green shirt, blue bandana and yellowish brown Nankeen trousers tucked carefully into the tops of black Hessian leg riding boots. About his waist was a broad black belt with a United States Cavalry buckle. A Colt Cavalry Model Peacemaker was butt forward in its high riding, flap topped military holster on the right side. Such a rig offered excellent protection from the elements for the weapon, but did not grant unhindered accessibility should it be required urgently.

After a creditable and honorable career in the Army of the United States, rising to the rank of major in the Cavalry,[1] Mosehan had resigned his commission to become manager of the already extensive Hashknife ranch in Arizona. As was the case during his military service, he had acquired a reputation for being honest and scrupulously fair in his dealings

---

1. Although we referred to Bertram Mosehan as "Captain" in the previous volumes of the *Waco* series and *Part Six, "Keep Good Temper Alive," J.T.'S HUNDREDTH,* we are informed by Alvin Dustine "Cap" Fog that the source from which we produced them was in error and the rank we now use is correct. J.T.E.

with others, but *very* strict when in contention with those who transgressed upon him or any property for which he was responsible.

Although the major was ostensibly visiting Marana to participate in a forthcoming sale of livestock, he had another reason. He had been requested by his employers to go to the town and meet with a Mr. Edward Jervis, but they had given no further information. Accepting that the matter must be of importance, he had made the journey as quickly as possible. What was more, on his arrival, he had made his way directly to the Pima County Hotel—where he had been told the man he was coming to see could be found—instead of first going to leave his horse at the livery barn. With the sale commencing the following morning, the small town was busy and clearly had numerous visitors. However, while passing along the main street and crossing the Spanish style *plaza* upon which the hotel stood—as did most of the main buildings—he had seen nobody he recognized from elsewhere.

Although failing to identify him, looking at the speaker, Mosehan had no doubt what he was. Tall-ish, lean, with shoulder long black hair and a vicious, unshaven face, his clothing was that of a cowhand. However, if the Colt Civilian Model Peacemaker he wore tied down and low heeled boots were any indication, any work he had been hired to do on a ranch was unlikely to have included handling the cattle. He was, unless the major guessed wrong, a hired gun fighter if not one of the top class.

"Have you?" Mosehan said quietly, his accent that of a Kansan; albeit one who had spent much of his life outside the State. Noticing that those people closest were backing away from what showed signs of developing into a most dangerous area, he stepped away from his horse to avoid putting it in jeopardy if—as seemed very likely—gunplay should take place. "Do you mind if I ask why?"

"You killed my brother," the man claimed, speaking louder than was necessary for just the major to hear.

"I did?" Mosehan queried, keeping his hands by his sides to prevent making anything which could be construed as a hostile gesture.

"Not personal, with your own hands," the man answered, right fist hovering over the butt of his revolver and eyes flickering to the closed flap of the holster worn by the major. "You didn't have the guts for that, so you got him hung for something you knowed damned well he didn't do."

"What was his name?" Mosehan asked.

During his Army service, circumstances had compelled the major to have three men hanged; but he was certain each had been guilty of the crimes with which they were charged!

"Joe Benedict," the man replied.

"*Benedict?*" Mosehan repeated, frowning in puzzlement. "I've never even *met* anybody called 'Benedict'."

"Liar!" the man shouted and grabbed for his gun.

Instead of trying to unfasten and open the flap of the Cavalry pattern holster, the major sent his right hand upward and across to the left. Passing beneath his unbuttoned jacket, it made a grasping and twisting motion. Then it emerged, holding a short barrelled Merwin & Hulbert Army Pocket revolver.

Confident that he had an unbeatable edge with his open topped fast draw rig, the man was startled by the unanticipated reaction from his intended victim. It caused him to hesitate for a vitally important instant in his otherwise rapidly flowing draw. When he resumed the movement of his right hand, such was his sense of haste, he over compensated. Although his Colt came clear and roared, the bullet missed its mark.

Showing no sign of being deterred or disconcerted by the lead passing so close he felt its wind on his cheek, Mosehan lined up the weapon he had produced. Thumbing back the hammer with the deft ease of long practice, as was required by the single action mechanism, he squeezed the trigger when satisfied with his instinctive chest high alignment. Flame and smoke erupted from the muzzle. Shot between the eyes, in testimony to his ability, the man twirled and, letting fall the Peacemaker, sprawled face downward on to the ground.

"By the gunsmith's, Major!" yelled a husky yet carrying masculine voice which sounded familiar. "Get down!"

Without waiting to find out whether he was correct in his assumption over the identity of the speaker, seeing a man carrying a Winchester rifle coming from the alley between the gunsmith's shop and another building, Mosehan carried out the advice. He realized, however, he was still in considerable danger regardless of the warning. Something over thirty yards separated them; a distance giving a shoulder arm a distinct advantage over a handgun, particularly a model with a barrel reduced to a length of three and five-sixteenths inches as an aid to concealment rather than range. While he was also carrying a Peacemaker which could have been more suitable to his needs, there would not be sufficient time allowed for him to draw and bring it into use.

Even as the major was drawing his unpalatable conclusions and starting to roll in the hope of taking at least partial shelter behind the lifeless man, he heard three shots. They had the deep bark of a heavy caliber revolver, not the sharper crack emitted by a rifle, and came from somewhere near the source of the voice which delivered the warning. Although none of the bullets took effect, as far as he could see, they caused the would-be attacker to have a change of mind. Spinning on his heel without offering to raise the rifle, he darted back in the direction from which he had come.

Rising and scanning the remainder of the plaza, Mosehan sought for any more companions of the man he had been compelled to kill. Satisfied there were none, he turned toward the hotel.

"You show up at the damnedest time, Pete," the major greeted, looking at the rescuer who was crossing the sidewalk carrying a smoking Remington New Model of 1874 Army revolver in his right fist. "Care to come with me after that jasper with the rifle?"

"He had a hoss down the alley and's already fogging out on it," replied the man who had intervened, his accent that of a New Yorker born in the already notorious East Side region. "Mine's down to the livery barn and that bay of yours doesn't look up to no fast chasing."

Regardless of a voice indicating he had been born and raised in the largest Eastern city, the speaker did not look in any way out of place in a small range country town. His multi-colored, tight rolled bandana, open necked tartan shirt, Levi's and boots were such as any working cowhand might wear. An off white Mexican *sombrero* dangled by its *barbiquejo* chinstrap on his shoulders, exposing a head of close cropped black hair. Swarthy in pigmentation, his rugged face had a disciplined strength relieved by the suggestion of a sense of humor. Of medium height, he had a barrel of a chest set on bulky hips and slightly bowed legs. As he was speaking, he returned the Remington to its cross draw holster. This was on the left side of a gunbelt which, although secured by a buckle similar to that of Mosehan's rig, had been made with the needs of a western gun fighter in mind and not those of a cavalry soldier.

"You're right about that," the major conceded, replacing the Merwin & Hulbert in the spring retention "half breed" shoulder holster from which it had come.

"Looks like leaving the Army hasn't stopped you finding trouble, major," Peter Glendon remarked, joining the man who had been his commanding officer on the street.

"It found me," Mosehan corrected. "Only I'll be damned if I know why. Do you recollect anybody called 'Joe Benedict' while we were serving together, Pete?"

"I can't bring any such to mind," Glendon confessed, after thinking for a few seconds, oblivious of the crowd who were gathering.

"That jasper said I had his brother hanged," Mosehan explained, indicating the body with a jerk of his thumb. "But none of the three were called 'Joe Benedict'."

"No," the stocky man agreed. "The two you arrested for raping and killing that Navajo girl were Buckton and Weighill and that snow-bird[2] who murdered the old prospector on the Yellowstone afore we tracked him down was called Joel Benskill. But we never had no doings with a feller called Benedict."

"And, unless he was using another name, I haven't come across one since I took over at the Hashknife," Mosehan declared. "Comes to a point, I haven't had

---

2. "Snow-bird" derogatory name given by soldiers to a man who enlists to obtain food, pay and shelter when winter approaches and intends to desert when the weather improves. J.T.E.

anybody hanged since those three either and every one of them was guilty."

"There's no god-damned doubt about that," Glendon confirmed, then gave a derisive sniff and continued, "Here come the local John Laws, on time as usual."

Glancing in the same direction as his former sergeant, Mosehan studied the two local enforcers of law and order who were pushing with scant courtesy through the onlookers. Both appeared to be in their early twenties and, being a shrewd judge of character, he was not impressed by what he saw even without the indication of disapproval displayed by Glendon.

Slightly the taller of the two, Jackson Martin clearly regarded himself as the leader. His surly features were set in a frown augmented by the moustache he cultivated to make him appear older. Longish black hair shown from beneath his round topped black hat. He wore a black cutaway coat, floral patterned vest, white shirt and black string tie. Striped trousers were tucked into the legs of his riding boots. Looking so glossy it might have been patent leather, his gunbelt carried two rosewood handled Colt Civilian Peacemakers in its fast draw holsters. A sawed off shotgun rested upon his bent right arm and the badge of a deputy sheriff glinted under the left lapel of the jacket.

No better looking, with a similar hirsute appendage on his top lip, Alfred "Leftie Alf" Dubs was brown haired and two years younger. His attire was much the same as that worn by Martin, but of cheaper material, and his Colts had plain walnut grips. Unlike his companion, he displayed his badge of office in plain view and was carrying his sawed off shotgun with his near hand grasping the wrist of its butt.

"What's happened here?" Martin demanded, halting and eyeing the two men arrogantly, his accent Mid-Western and suggesting a good education.

"That man tried to kill me," Mosehan replied quietly, nodding to the body. "And I stopped him."

"It looks that way," Martin admitted and something of his arrogance left in the presence of a man he sensed could not be browbeaten by virtue of his civic authority. "Who is he?"

"I don't know," the major declared. "That's the damnedest thing about it. He claimed I'd had his brother hanged, but the name he gave doesn't come to mind."

"You hanged so many men you can't remember them all?" challenged Dubs, in a voice suggesting he came from the same region as his companion, albeit his origins were lower on the social scale.

"I said I'd had hanged, not that I'd hanged them," Mosehan corrected coldly. "There's a difference. Anyways, whoever he was, he had a feller backing him. Sergeant Glendon here cut in and that one ran away down the alley."

"Why didn't you take out after him?" Dubs wanted to know, being less susceptible to atmosphere than the other deputy.

"We thought your *superior* would prefer for us to stay here until he'd heard what happened," the major explained with a studied politeness which his former sergeant recognized as a danger sign. "Is he coming?"

"*I'm* in charge of the sheriff's office here and double as town marshal!" Martin announced stiffly, emphasizing the first word. "Go and look for the one who ran away, Leftie."

"Sure, Jackson!" Dubs assented, but with more reluctance than cheerful acceptance of an order.

"Now was it me going after a feller," Glendon commented dryly. "I'd want to know what he looked like."

"What did he look like?" Martin growled, as the other deputy stopped his intended departure, hearing chuckles from the onlookers.

"Tallish, with a high crowned white hat, and black vest," the stocky man supplied. "Took off on a roan hoss, but I didn't see which way he turned when he got to the end of the alley over there."

"You best go ask around if anybody did see, Leftie!" Martin ordered, his sallow face reddening. Showing no sign of knowing Glendon was present, he turned his gaze to the major and asked authoritatively, "Who are you?"

"Bertram Mosehan," was the quiet reply.

"Mose—!" the taller deputy began. Then, being aware of the influential people who employed the man he was questioning, he adopted a more polite attitude. "I don't think there's anything to keep you here, Major Mosehan, it was a clear case of self defense."

"Thank you," Mosehan answered, with just a trace of irony. "I'll be here for a few days, probably, in case you need me for anything."

"I'll keep it in mind," Martin promised and looked around. "Hey, some of you fellers carry the body to the undertaker's parlor for me."

"Do you mind if I drop by at your office to look through the wanted dodgers?" the major asked, as the instruction was being obeyed by members of the crowd. "I'd like to find out who he is."

"I'll do that for you," Martin offered.

"Thanks," Mosehan answered. "I reckon I owe you a drink for cutting in the way you did, Pete."

"Which I've never been known to refuse since I was big enough to pick up a beer stein," Glendon assented.

"Who are those two knobheads?" Mosehan inquired, as he and his former sergeant crossed the sidewalk to enter the hotel.

"Names are Martin and Dubs," the stocky man replied. "Figure they're wild, woolly and so full of fleas they've never been curried below the knees."

"I got the notion you don't cotton to them."

"I've met snow-birds and sheep herders I'm better took with."

"How's that?"

"Way they act, particularly Martin, they must reckon to be another couple of Wyatt Earps," Glendon snorted.

"Do they?" Mosehan said dryly. "I've heard tell

there are people who say *one* Wyatt Earp is way too many."

"And I'm one of them," Glendon claimed. "Don't know if you know it, Major, but I'm ramrodding the Cross Bar Cross out of town a ways. Soon's they come in here after the old deputy retired, Martin and his bunkie showed they was figuring to pull some of those Kansas fighting pimp games on the local cowhands. I sort of talked them out of the notion, 'specially where my crew was concerned."

"That's why they looked like they wished you weren't there," Mosehan decided with a grin, remembering how effectively his former sergeant could handle either a rough-house brawl or a gun. Having entered and crossed the bar room while they were talking and coming to a halt at the counter, he went on, "Name your poison, Pete."

"Bourbon, happen that's all right with you, Major, I've got sort of high-toned tastes since I was made foreman," the stocky man replied and, after the order had been given to the bartender, continued, "Are you in town for the cattle sales?"

"That's why my bosses said I should let on I'd come here," Mosehan answered.

"Excuse me," a voice said, before the explanation could be completed. "Are you Major Bertram Mosehan?"

Turning from the counter, the two cattlemen looked the speaker up and down. Clad in a somber black suit, white shirt with a collar which appeared to endanger his prominent adam's apple by its stiffness, a black cravat and blunt toed boots, he was balding, middle-sized, slender and had an obsequious demeanor. Although his attire was of a somewhat better quality than was usually the case, he reminded them of business clerks they had come across who a lifetime of yielding to the wishes of those higher in the office hierarchy had left—although neither knew, much less expressed, the term—suffering from a marked inferiority complex.

"I am," Mosehan confirmed.

"His Hon—*Mr. Jervis* is in his room and would like you to join him as soon as it is convenient," the newcomer announced, something in his manner implying the invitation should be accepted immediately even if not convenient.

"I don't think you and I have met," the major hinted.

"We haven't, sir," the man admitted. "My name is Erroll Madden."

"Will our business take long, Mr. Madden?" Mosehan asked.

"Possibly, sir," the man replied vaguely. "I couldn't say for sure."

"In that case," Mosehan said, suspecting Madden had the type of mentality which would refuse to offer further information unless it could be done so in the guise of conferring a favor. It was a point of view which he had come across many times throughout his military career and he had never regarded it favorably. However, past experiences had taught him how to cope with such a mind and, giving a well simulated shrug of disinterest, he went on, "I'll go and bed down my horse before I see him."

"His—*He* did stress the urgency of the situation," Madden protested.

"I'll see to your hoss for you, major," Glendon offered, despite knowing what his former commanding officer was up to. "I want to go take a look at mine, I left him getting shod."

"That's good of you, Pete," Mosehan praised, being intrigued by the possibility of learning why he had been instructed to make the journey from the Hashknife ranch, and coming to a conclusion from the way in which the miserable looking man referred to "Mr. Jervis." However, although for once he was willing to forego attending to his horse—knowing it would be in good hands—he could not resist continuing, "I'll come and fetch my bedroll, then see if I can get a room."

"There is a room booked for you already," Madden claimed, showing agitation over the possibility of a delay. "And a bellboy will take your—bedroll—to it for you."

"By cracky, why didn't I think of *that*?" Mosehan ejaculated. "Can you give the bedroll to him before you go, Pete?"

"Sure."

"*Gracias!*"

"*Es nada,*" the stocky ranch foreman replied amiably. "And when you get through, maybe we can get together in here to bend an elbow a couple or so times in memory of the boys of good old Company A?"

"I'd like nothing more than that," Mosehan affirmed, with genuine warmth although this left his voice as he concluded, "All right, Mr. Madden, let's go and see Mr. Jervis."

Chapter 6

I NEED GOOD MEN TO BACK ME

~~~

"WELL, WHAT DO YOU KNOW ABOUT THAT, PETE?" Major Bertram Mosehan asked, as his former sergeant crossed to meet him when he entered the bar room of the Pima County Hotel some ninety minutes after having left it with Erroll Madden. " 'Mr. Jervis' turns out to be the Governor of Arizona Territory and he wants me to become a peace officer."

"Doesn't he know you're pretty well fixed already and on something a whole heap safer 'n' better paid than that?" Peter Glendon inquired, showing no discernible emotion over the information, although his erstwhile commanding officer could tell he found it most interesting.

"Seems my bosses recommended me and are holding open my position at the Hashknife outfit until I get through," Mosehan replied, glancing around the room to find it had acquired many more customers in his absence. However, as had been the case when he was passing through Marana on his way to the rendezvous with "Mr. Jervis," he saw nobody other than Glendon with whom he was acquainted. "Let's find somewhere we can talk this out, Pete, unless you've anything needing to be done."

"I don't have," the stocky foreman of the Cross Bar Cross ranch asserted and made a gesture with his right hand. "We'll use that table over by the window."

"How about those fellers who're at it?"

"They ride for my outfit. Likely they'll take pity on their poor old ramrod and let me have it for just the two of us."

"Seems you haven't changed a bit, Pete," Mosehan claimed, a few seconds later, as he took a seat at the table by the window and watched the cowhands who had occupied it making their way to the bar.

"I sure haven't," Glendon agreed. "It's all done by kindness."

"And saying they'll wind up on k.p.?"[1] the major suggested.

"Not since I left the Cavalry," the former sergeant replied, also grinning. "Now all I do is tell them I need somebody to ride the blister end of a shovel."

---

1. "K.p.": abbreviation for "kitchen police," the name given in the Army of the United States for enlisted men assigned to assist the cooks, or carry out other menial duties, as a form of minor punishment. J.T.E.

"I never asked how you came to be on hand just when I needed it, Pete," Mosehan remarked, noticing Madden looking at him through the door from the lobby and then turn to disappear in the direction of the front entrance to the hotel. "How was it?"

"I was sitting here with the boys when I saw you coming across the plaza," Glendon explained, signalling for one of the waiters. "So I headed on out to say, 'howdy.' Only you looked a mite busy when I got to the front door and I figured to keep watch in case you needed backing. Seemed like you did when I saw that yahoo with the rifle, so I concluded I'd best cut in."

"I'm obliged you did," the major stated. "*Gracias* again."

"Like I said before, *es nada,*" the foreman replied, the Spanish term meaning, "it was nothing" sounding somewhat strange in conjunction with his Brooklyn accent. Then, after the waiter had come to take their order and delivered it, he asked, "Why'd they pick you 'special' to pin a badge on? No disrespect meant, mind, only there's a whole slew of fellers in Arizona Territory and through the rest of the West, comes to that, who don't do nothing but peace officering."

"That's what I told 'Mr. Jervis'," Mosehan admitted, glancing through the window at the people passing along the sidewalk. "But it seems none of the men he considers most suitable is able to come right now and he doesn't think any of those he can lay hands on around the Territory would do what he needs."

"Including the Earps?"

"*Particularly* the Earps."

"Well, you won't hear me, nor any other cowhand, complaining 'cause he counts the Earps among them he *doesn't* want," Glendon declared with vehemence. "It's the first time I ever knowed a politician do anything which showed good sense." Raising his glass and sipping as if drinking a toast to the wisdom of "Mr. Jervis," he set it down again and became more serious as he continued, "Only it cuts deeper than you just being asked to put on a badge, don't it?"

"It does," Mosehan confirmed. "You've heard about that business up in Coconino County?"

"You mean about that 'mother-something' Eastern shyster threatening to sue the sheriff for grabbing and fetching back those bank robbers from outside his bailiwick?"

"That's what I mean, Pete. It's got 'Mr. Jervis' real worried. He's committed to trying to have Statehood granted to Arizona, but there's too much lawlessness going on right now for Congress to be willing to move that way."

"Making sheriffs quit going outside their bailiwick after owlhoots ain't what I'd call the right way to set about stopping law breaking!"

"It isn't," Mosehan conceded, having heard similar sentiments from numerous other law abiding citizens since news of the events in Coconino County was made public. "The trouble is, that's the law of these United States. It's just that until now no smart-assed, legal-wrangling, son-of-a-bitch has thought to use that law."

"God damn it!" the foreman ejaculated, banging his clenched right fist on the table. However, he was sufficiently in control of himself to hold down his voice as he went on, "Can that son-of-a-bitch get away with it?"

"*That's* the question, Pete," the major said, just as quietly, deciding retirement had not caused his former sergeant to lose a well developed sense of discretion. "You and 'Mr. Jervis' both would like to know the answer. Word of what's going on has spread well beyond Arizona and a whole slew of people are waiting to see how things turn out. That's particularly the case with those who are against Statehood being granted, they'll be ready to use it no matter which way things go."

"With that kind," Glendon said bitterly, "it's always a case of, 'Heads, I win, tails, you lose.' "

"You're as right as the off side of a horse," Mosehan admitted. "Anyways, the Governor's passed word to every sheriff and town marshal in the Territory not to go outside his bailiwick after outlaws until the Supreme Court has handed down its ruling."

"Then why'd he send for you?"

"To form a force of peace officers who *will* have the authority to go everywhere in Arizona regardless of city limits, or county lines."

"You mean like the Texas Rangers?"

"Like the Texas Rangers," Mosehan confirmed.

"Except that we'll be able to go in and do what needs doing without needing to wait to be asked by the local officers."[2]

"Sounds interesting," Glendon remarked, in what some people might have considered a casual fashion.

"I need good men to back me," Mosehan announced, as he did not come into the above category. "Of course, I wouldn't want to ask a feller who's settled down as the foreman of a ranch to sit in—!"

"My boss'll be just as willing as your'n to hold my job should I be *told* to do something like this," the foreman claimed, still in the same completely disinterested sounding tone. "He's real keen on seeing Arizona made a State."

"Are you volunteering to join?" Mosehan inquired, with seeming innocence.

"*Volunteering!*" Glendon repeated, sounding as if the word left a bad taste in his mouth. "Did you ever know a thirty-year non-com to *volunteer* for anything, major?"

"You know something, Pete, I don't believe I ever did," Mosehan said with a smile, delighted to have received the unspoken offer and equally grateful for the good fortune which had brought himself and his for-

---

2. Although, as is told in *A TOWN CALLED YELLOWDOG* an investigation might occasionally be launched without an official invitation, the Texas Rangers were expected to wait until called in by the local law enforcement agency concerned before participating in an investigation, or pursuit of criminals. However, during the Prohibition Era, Company "Z" was formed and authorized to take whatever action might prove necessary to prevent law breakers escaping the consequences of their actions by loopholes in the legal system. See the *Alvin Dustine "Cap" Fog* series for details. J.T.E.

mer sergeant together at such a propitious moment. "How would it be if I asked you to lend a hand?"

"I'd be likely to have the vapors was a field officer like you to *ask* me to do something," Glendon declared, so somberly he might have been in deadly earnest. "Why don't you give me an *order*, like always, major?"

"All right, sergeant!" Mosehan obliged, his voice taking on a clipped and authoritative timber. "Haul your butt away from the easy living at the Cross Bar Cross and get ready to do some *work* for a change."

"Yo!" the former sergeant assented, as he would have done during his military service when receiving such a command from an officer he respected.

"I can take on a dozen or so men," the major announced, getting down to the more serious business even though a stranger would have been hard put to tell there was anything different in his demeanor and way of speaking. "Have you any suggestions?"

"Got Fast Billy Cromaty on the payroll at the spread, happen you remember him?"

"That lanky, carrot-headed young cuss I made corporal on the Yellowstone?"

"That's him."

"He'll do," Mosehan confirmed, remembering the man in question to be far more intelligent than he looked and generally acted.

"There are four-five more of the boys from Company A around the Territory I can bring in," Glendon offered.

"Do that," the major authorized, being willing to accept the judgment of his erstwhile non-com. "You'll take rank as sergeant and I've a couple of men at the Hashknife I'll ask to join."

"We'll still be some short even if they'll all take on," Glendon estimated.

"Then we'll have to look around for others," Mosehan replied. "I know the kind of men I want, but finding them won't be easy."

The sound of a commotion from outside the hotel brought the conversation to a halt!

Turning his head, the major looked through the window to where half a dozen young cowhands were strolling along the sidewalk. From all appearances, they were celebrating their visit to the town. Laughing, talking loudly, occasionally letting out whoops of joy and jostling one another, they were behaving in a rowdy yet good humored fashion. Among them was one he recognized.

Tall and so lanky as to be almost skeletal, William "Fast Billy" Cromaty[3] had a spikey mop of hair—the orange-red of a carrot—which no amount of combing, or application of patent lotions, could keep under control for more than a few minutes. Such was the vacant expression on his excessively freckled ruddy face, people meeting him for the first time fre-

---

3. Due to a further error in the source of information from which we produced the earlier volumes of the *Waco* series, we gave the name, "Billy Speed" to William "Fast Billy" Cromaty. We apologize to the descendants of the former for any inconvenience this mistake may have caused. J.T.E.

quently assumed he was slow witted. Dressed in his "go to town" finery, the shirt and bandana were of such clashing and far from tasteful hues, they might have suggested he was color blind. However, although he seemed awkward and slothful, he could both move and think quickly enough when the need arose. More than one person had discovered how well he could handle himself in an all-in brawl and he was just as capable with the Colt Civilian Model Peacemaker on his gunbelt.

On the point of rapping upon the window to attract the attention of Cromaty, Mosehan saw one of the happy group push another. As he was sent stumbling forward, the head of the cowhand suddenly jerked and the temple on the side nearest the hotel burst open. Having passed through, a bullet shattered the pane and hissed between the seated pair. Fortunately also missing the other occupants of the bar room, it ended its flight in the front of the counter. Rising with such haste and vehemence they sent the chairs pitching behind them, the major and Glendon watched what was happening outside.

The stricken cowhand reeled to crash his shoulders through the window, but slid to the sidewalk instead of tumbling onward into the bar room!

Startled exclamations burst from the rest of the group!

Of all the cowhands, Cromaty reacted most swiftly and effectively!

Spinning outward, bringing the Colt from its holster

with the kind of speed which had earned him the sobriquet, "Fast Billy," the lanky cowhand set off across
the plaza at a run in no way slothful or awkward!

"What the—?" Glendon began.

"Come on!" Mosehan snapped. "Billy's going after
whoever did the shooting!"

Ignoring the questions directed at them by the customers and employees of the hotel, the two men ran
from the bar room. Equally oblivious to the requests
for information they received while going through
the lobby, they made for the front entrance. On
reaching the sidewalk, they found the other
cowhands staring either at the dead man, or across
the open space to where Cromaty was already approaching the alley from which the man with the rifle
had appeared after Mosehan had shot his intended
killer on arriving in Marana.

Reaching the gap between the gunsmith's shop and
a general store, the lanky cowhand saw the man who
had killed his companion at the other end of the
buildings. Even if there had been others in the alley,
he could have made the recognition from the manner
in which the other was dressed and the way in which
the Winchester Model of 1873 rifle was being held
while the owner was gathering up the dangling reins
of a "ground hitched" horse. Any lingering doubts
would have been removed by the way the man behaved on glancing in his direction. Allowing the reins
to slip from his grip, he swiveled around and started
to raise the rifle toward a firing position.

Skidding to a halt, Cromaty realized the distance was too great for him to attempt firing at waist level and by instinctive alignment. With his left hand joining the right on the butt, he swung up the Colt at arms' length to a height where he could make use of its somewhat rudimentary sights. Taking aim swiftly, he cut loose. Regardless of the speed with which it was discharged, the bullet flew true. Caught in the left breast an instant before he was ready to use the rifle, pain caused the man to toss it aside and he went over backward.

Cocking the Peacemaker on its recoil kick, the lanky cowhand resumed his interrupted advance. He went slowly, his attitude wary and he was ready to use the weapon again if necessary despite having allowed its barrel to sink and removing his left hand. The need for further action did not arise. Sprawled upon his back, heart torn apart by the two hundred and thirty grain, .45 caliber cone of lead, the man was dead by the time he came up. Hearing running footsteps to his rear, he allowed the Colt to dangle by his right thigh and turned.

"Pete!" Cromaty greeted, his normally lethargic Kentucky drawl showing relief. Then, recognizing the second of the men who led the small crowd along the alley, he went on, "Hey, it's *you*, Maj'!"

"It is, Billy," Mosehan confirmed and nodded toward the body. "Who is he?"

"I've never seed him afore," Cromaty replied.

"I have, by god!" Glendon snapped, looking down

at the black vest worn by the killer then to the high crowned white hat which had been knocked off as he fell and the Winchester rifle. "He's the same son-of-a-bitch who tried to cut in after you'd made wolf bait of that jasper outside the hotel, major."

"Are you sure?" Mosehan inquired, his view of the man in question having been of necessity restricted.

"Close enough," the foreman growled. "He'd dressed the same, the right build and got him a Winchester."

"That he has," the major agreed, remembering the description given to the two young peace officers. "Are you sure you don't know him, Billy?"

"Like I said, I've never seen the son-of-a-bitch afore," Cromaty asserted definitely, holstering his Colt. "What the hell could he have had again' a real friendly 'n' likeable kid like Terry?"

"I don't reckon he had anything," Glendon said quietly, after glancing at Mosehan.

"Hell, Pete!" the lanky cowhand protested. "Folks don't go around just shooting other folks for no reason!"

"He'd got a reason," the foreman replied. "But it wasn't Tommy he was after."

"Then who—?" Cromaty began.

"He was after *me*," Mosehan supplied, having reached similar conclusions to those drawn by Glendon.

"*You*, maj'?" the lanky cowhand queried. "But you wasn't on the sidewalk, nor in the plaza."

"I was sitting in the hotel, by the window you boys were passing," Mosehan explained. "Only Terry was pushed into the way just as that feller squeezed off at me."

"I wonder if he was kin to that yahoo you cut down, major?" Glendon inquired, but the question went unanswered.

Although a number of people had entered the alley, they had respected the signal Mosehan had given for them to stand back. However, at that moment, the peace officers arrived. As on the previous occasion, they shoved their way through the crowd in an officiously truculent fashion.

"It's you, major!" Deputy Sheriff Jackson Martin said, his truculent demeanor diminishing somewhat. "What happened this time?"

"That jasper who lit out last time came back for another try," Glendon answered, before Mosehan could reply.

"The one I went looking for?" asked Deputy Sheriff Alfred "Leftie Alf" Dubs.

"The identical, very same one," the foreman declared.

"But a feller I met told me he'd seen him riding out of town," Dubs objected.

"Which, looks like, he right soon came back," the foreman asserted, suspecting the peace officer had not continued the search after receiving the information.

"Why would he?" Dubs challenged.

"To try and finish what he'd run out on doing," Glendon replied, not trying to conceal his asperity. "Or to get even for his *amigo*."

"Or he could have been after revenge over that feller you ha—had hanged, major, like the other one," Martin suggested, throwing a prohibitive glare at the other peace officer while amending the words from, "you hanged" to "had hanged" as being more politic.

"That must have been it," Mosehan said, before Glendon could speak. "I should thank you for downing him, Billie. Looks like you're still as good with a gun as when I made you corporal on the Yellowstone."

"He'd put down Terry, maj'," Cromaty answered, seeing the deputies had not overlooked the reference to his having served with Mosehan in the Army. "I don't need no thanks for taking him out, I only wished I could've done it so he died slow and pained."

"You'd no choice but stop him dead, he was fixing to do the same to you," the major asserted. "What do you say, deputy?"

"He did what needed doing," Martin conceded, albeit grudgingly as he disliked cowhands in general and had failed to browbeat Cromaty on the one occasion he tried, but judging the answer he gave the most suitable under the circumstances.

"See to the body, please," Mosehan said, although the words sounded closer to an order than a request.

"We'll go and take care of the young man he killed while he was trying for me."

Allowing the deputies no chance to agree with or raise objections to his instructions, the major turned and set off along the alley accompanied by Glendon and Cromaty.

"What do you reckon, major?" the foreman inquired, as the trio entered the plaza. "Because it's way short of what you told those two knobheads."

"I don't think that first man was after me for what he said," Mosehan replied. "He just used it for what would pass as a good reason to call me down. That's why he claimed his 'brother's' name was 'Joe Benedict.' He'd heard about the hangings, or whoever hired him had, but got Joel Benskill's name mixed. A man wouldn't do that if he was talking about his brother."

"Then it must be somebody you've riled since you've been running the Hashknife outfit," Glendon guessed.

"They were waiting for me *here*," Mosehan pointed out. "Apart from the owners, nobody knew I was coming and I couldn't have been followed closely enough to have been ridden around and beaten into town without me seeing whoever was doing the following."

"Likely not," the foreman conceded. "Which, sounds to me, somebody knew why you were coming and doesn't take kindly to you doing like the Gov— 'Mr. Jervis' has in mind."

Before any more could be said, a stagecoach entered the plaza!

This, the local men knew was out of the ordinary!

Although the depot of the Arizona State Stage Line was two doors along from the hotel, the vehicles normally went around the rear to where the stables were situated. Furthermore, there were signs that something was amiss. A tall, blond, young Texan was seated on the box alongside the driver. Three saddled horses were fastened by lead ropes to the rear boot and, lashed to the roof, was what could only be a human body wrapped in a tarpaulin sheet.

"Looks like they hit trouble," Cromaty suggested, almost dreamily it would have seemed to any stranger who had overheard him. "That's not Walt Tract's regular shotgun messenger riding with him."

"We'd best find out what's happened," Mosehan decided.

"Sure," Glendon agreed. "Could be this's the start of our first chore."

Chapter 7

YOU KNOW BELLE STAR *REAL* WELL

❧

"BELLE STARR, YOU SAY?" DEPUTY SHERIFF JACKSON Martin ejaculated briskly, as Walter Tract concluded his description of the hold up. "We'd best get up a posse and go after her, Alf!"

"The sooner the better, Jackson," Deputy Alfred "Leftie Alf" Dubs agreed, showing an unusual eagerness to carry out his duties and also ignoring the fact that night would have fallen long before the scene of the incident could be reached. Darting a glance redolent of annoyance at the driver, he went on, "There's been enough time wasted already."

While Doc Leroy had worked upon the injuries of the shotgun messenger, hoping his diagnosis and decision over the treatment was correct, Tract had helped to wrap the body of Maurice Blenheim in the tarpaulin and load it securely on the roof of the stagecoach. Then, acting under the crisp and decisive orders of the pallid faced Texan, the center seat was lowered and, having been swaddled in a blanket from Doc's bedroll to prevent him moving when he recovered consciousness, Benjamin Eckland had been placed upon it. With this done to his satisfaction, Doc had stated his intention of riding at the side of his patient.

Tying the horses he and his companion were using to the supports of the baggage boot at the rear of the vehicle, Waco had suggested he "ride shotgun" on the box and Tract had agreed. However, despite having loaded the Greener, he had supplemented his brace of staghorn handled Colt Artillery Model Peacemakers with the rifle from his saddleboot. This had proved to be one of the recently introduced .45–75 caliber Winchester Model of 1876, heavier and, taking a powder load of seventy-five grains as opposed to the forty used in the Model of 1873, more powerful than its predecessors from that manufacturer. On the driver commenting it was the first of its kind he had seen, the blond replied he had purchased it during a visit to Chicago, but did not go into further details.[1]

With the surviving passengers inside the vehicle, Jedroe Franks having retrieved his Colt Storekeeper

---

1. Why the visit was paid is told in: *WACO'S DEBT.* J.T.E.

Model Peacemaker and Pierre Henri Jaqfaye the walking stick, the journey had been resumed. Bearing in mind what Doc had told him about Eckland's physical condition and the bluntly spoken instructions he received, which had clearly not met with the approval of Senator Paul Michael Twelfinch II although no protest was registered vocally, Tract had concentrated all his skill upon making the ride into Marana as smooth as possible. Doing so precluded carrying out any lengthy conversation and, as had been the case while preparing the body for transportation, Waco had learned little about what had taken place during the hold up. Nor had he made any comment on the one occasion the subject had briefly arisen when the driver had mentioned the supposition of the woman's identity.

Although Tract had brought the stagecoach through the plaza on arriving at the town, it had not been so that he could go directly to the jailhouse which also served as an office for the municipal and county law enforcement agencies. Nor had he drawn rein on approaching the building used as a depot by the Arizona State Stage Line. Instead, he had kept moving until reaching the premises in which the local doctor maintained a surgery. Bringing the vehicle to a stop, he had helped to carry Eckland inside. Then, leaving Doc with the shotgun messenger, he had driven on once more until reaching the stables and corral behind the depot, as would have happened without the detour if the journey had been uneventful. Not until the hostlers were starting to attend to his horses, sharing the small regard of Peter Glendon for the abilities and habits of the two young deputies, had he sent word for them.

By the time Martin and Dubs arrived, for once having a genuine reason for the delay in putting in their appearance, the body was unloaded and a small group of curious people had assembled. Although the foreman of the Cross Bar Cross ranch and William "Fast Billy" Cromaty were present, Major Bertram Mosehan was not with them. As he had been on the point of accompanying them, he had seen the Governor of Arizona Territory standing on the first floor balcony of the Pima County Hotel. Clearly wishing to find out what had caused the commotion on the sidewalk below his suite of rooms, an innovation of which the owners of the establishment were very proud as such a facility was by no means common in small towns, "Mr. Jervis" had signalled for Mosehan to join him. Telling the other two to follow the stagecoach and authorizing Glendon to inform the lanky cowhand of the proposal which had been made to him, the major had gone to obey the summons. On hearing of it, as Mosehan and Glendon had guessed would be the case, Cromaty had offered to enroll in the new and, as yet, unnamed law enforcement agency.

Modelling his behavior upon that he attributed to his hero, Wyatt Earp, including a penchant for "grandstanding" before the public—although he had not yet gone to the extreme of obtaining a Peace-maker with a barrel sixteen inches in length and which had already acquired, if not officially as far as the manufacturers were concerned,[2] the nickname, "Buntline Special"—Martin had set about demon-strating that he was taking charge by arrogantly de-manding to be told what had happened.

"I don't think it was Belle Starr," Franks put in.

"*You* don't, huh?" Martin sniffed, looking the be-spectacled and apparently unarmed young passenger over from head to foot in obvious disdain. "And here am I thinking, from what the driver told us about her being blonde, beautiful, with a real good shape and a Southern accent you could cut with a knife, how well she fits the descriptions I've seen of Belle Starr."

"And, the way he told it," Dubs went on, no less offensively. "The rest of the gang as good as named her more than once."

"That's one of the things which makes me doubt if she really is Belle Starr," Franks claimed, his cheeks reddening. Conscious that Waco, Tract and Jaqfaye in particular were paying greater attention and dis-playing less skepticism than either of the peace offi-cers or others in his audience, he continued, "From what I've read about her, Belle Starr is too smart to

2. Not until 1955, as a result of actor Hugh O'Brien carrying such a weapon while starring in the television series, WYATT EARP, which aroused the interest and a demand from the viewing public, did the Colt Manufacturing Company produce a Single Action Army revolver—albeit with a barrel only twelve inches in length—which they distributed as the "Buntline Special." J.T.E.

pick men who would make such a slip even once, much less as often as it happened today. What was more, her accent wasn't consistent and she said, 'you-all' far more than any Southron I've met."

"Is *that* all?" Dubs asked, clearly discounting everything he had heard as being of no importance.

"No," Franks replied, forcing himself to control his rising temper. "When I mentioned Calamity Jane beating Belle Starr when they had their fight at Butte, Montana, she said it was the other way around."

"Way she told it, though," Tract injected, although he had a feeling that something was wrong. "It came out like she'd slipped up and nearly said, 'me' then changed it to 'Belle Starr.' "

"According to how I read it, the fight ended in a draw," Franks commented, but was not allowed to finish.

"You don't reckon Belle Starr would want even *you* to go on thinking she was whipped by Calamity Jane, do you?" Dubs demanded derisively, glancing for appreciation of his ready grasp of the situation from the onlookers.

"Probably she wouldn't," Franks conceded. "But she should have known the fight took place at Elkhorn and not Butte."[3]

"By cracky, *yes!*" the driver ejaculated, as the real-

---

3. The fight and what led up to it is described in: *Part One, "The Bounty On Belle Starr's Scalp," TROUBLED RANGE* and, with added facts subscribed by Alvin Dustine "Cap" Fog and Andrew Mark "Big Andy" Counter, q.v., the "expansion" of the episode entitled: *CALAMITY, MARK AND BELLE.* J.T.E.

ization of what he had suspected to be wrong arrived. "It was *Elkhorn* where they locked horns."

"If I was pulling a hold up, I wouldn't be paying all that much close attention to something like that," Dubs asserted bombastically. "Hell, everybody *knows* Belle Starr has a couple of half-breeds riding in her gang."

"Blue *Duck* and *Sammy* Crane," Waco supplied, laying noticeable emphasis on the surname of the first outlaw and the Christian name of the second.

"That's what she called th—!" Tract began, then slapped his right hand against his off thigh. "By grab, no it wasn't though! They was called Blue *Buck* and *Tommy* Crane, as I recall it."

"So they were!" Franks agreed. "And, while I can't claim to have met too many of the real thing, those two sounded like actors in a melodrama playing the part of half breeds. The one called 'Tommy Crane' lost his accent once and, hard as he talked most of the time, he acted *very* squeamish when it came to taking the money belt from the man they killed. What is more, while it probably doesn't prove anything one way or another, neither of them toed inward when they were walking like I've read Indians always do."

"Sounds like you must do a whole slew of reading, *dude*," Dubs mocked. "And, from the way you've been sprouting off, here I was thinking you know Belle Starr *real* well."

"*Hombre*," Waco drawled and something in his

apparently lazy speech prevented Franks from making the heated response which begged to be uttered. "Take it from me this gent's making right good sense, from here to there and back the hard way, what he's saying—Which *I* know Belle Starr real well."

"Well now," Martin commented, not caring for the way in which the other deputy was dominating the conversation. "That's not a thing many folks would care to come out and admit so openly, considering what she and her gang have done."

"You mean what a woman who made out to be her and her gang did," the blond Texan corrected.

"If just *made out* is *all* it was," Martin answered.

"That's that," Waco conceded, with the air of one conferring a favor. "Only I mind one time somebody mistook me for Bad Bill Longley. Way things stood,[4] I didn't say no different and I'd be willing to bet there's folks in that town will reckon they met Bad Bill and not me."

"Is that so?" Martin growled, his temper rising as he saw he had not elicited the support from the crowd which he hoped would be forthcoming when he referred to what had happened during the hold up. "There's not many who'd want to be mistaken for a back shooting killer like him."

"I said *Bill Longley,*" the blond countered, drawing conclusions from the way in which the man he was addressing was clothed and behaved. "Not Wyatt Earp!"

4. Told in: *Part Two, "A Second Case Of Mistaken Identity," THE TEXAN.* J.T.E.

"Don't you mean-mouth Mr. Earp, you god-damned beef-head!" Martin spat out, employing the derogatory term for a Texan and making a start at bringing the sawed-off shotgun from across the crook of his right arm.

Taking a rapid stride forward, Waco reached with both hands to grasp the weapon. As he did so, he kept moving until alongside the deputy at the right. Swiftly hooking his right leg behind Martin's knees, he pushed forward with his arms. Caught totally unawares by the speed and strength with which the response was delivered, the peace officer could not prevent himself from being overbalanced. Feeling himself falling, a mixture of panic and instinct led him to release the shotgun. While this served to complete what Waco had begun, he contrived to go down in a sitting position instead of falling on to his back.

Seeing what was happening, Dubs snarled a profanity and prepared to take a hand. Unlike his companion, he had left his shotgun at the office when being informed they were needed behind the stage line's depot. However, despite the rapidity with which the Texan was moving, he considered he could cope without needing it. Having drawn this conclusion, he sent his right hand toward its holstered Colt.

Showing satisfaction over being granted an excuse, Franks whipped off the spectacles with his left hand. Holding them, he lunged forward. Inclining his torso downward, he wrapped his arms around the legs of the deputy. An instant later, his shoulder rammed into the other's midsection. Winded by the impact, Dubs was bent across his assailant and he was unable to complete his draw. Instead, he felt himself lifted and thrust to the rear, then released. Although he alighted on his feet, this proved of no advantage. The impetus he had been given by the man he had dismissed as a weak and harmless dude caused him to reel a few blundering steps in the direction of some of the onlookers. If a more popular peace officer had been involved, they would have helped him to come to a halt. Indicative of how he was regarded, those who could have been of assistance moved aside and allowed him to topple supine between them. In one respect, he was less fortunate than the other deputy as the landing knocked all the breath from his body.

Spitting out almost incoherent expletives, Martin glared up at his intended victim for a moment!

Then the furious deputy grabbed for the revolver in his right side holster!

Allowing the shotgun to fall, Waco's hands made a blurring motion!

Practically at the same instant, just over half a second after the movement commenced and before the discarded weapon reached the ground, the staghorn handled Colt Artillery Model Peacemakers rose above the lips of their respective holsters. To the accompaniment of a clicking, as the hammers were thumbed back to the fully cocked position, the five and a half inch long barrels turned forward. Seeming far larger than their caliber of .45 of an inch, the muzzles were pointed directly at the suddenly shocked and paling face of the seated deputy.

A concerted gasp arose from the crowd, in echo to that given by Martin!

Like the deputy, every man present knew they had just witnessed a superlative exhibition of gun handling!

There was, however, one very important difference from the point of view of the crowd and that of Martin!

While the interest of the onlookers was merely academic, the deputy knew he had never been in greater peril!

Martin was aware that many men who went through the long and gruelling hours of training needed to acquire such rapidity did not possess an excessive belief in the sanctity of human life when applied to others. There were some of their number—not excluding his hero, Wyatt Earp—who would have no hesitation over allowing the hammers of the revolvers to fall after having received such provocation. Nor would any of the onlookers offer to intercede on his behalf.

At that moment, the deputy regretted having created so much hostility while in office and wished he was the kind of respected peace officer who would receive the support of the population.

The shots anticipated—dreaded even—by Martin were not fired!

"Hombre," the blond said, his voice as apparently

innocuous as the first whispering murmur of a Texas "blue norther" storm, after what seemed to the frightened deputy to have extended far longer than the five or so seconds which actually passed. "I could've called *that* bet just's easy as your other." Having made the comment, he allowed the hammers to descend under control and twirled his Colts back into leather almost as quickly as they had left. Then, glancing to where Franks was donning the spectacles, he grinned and said, *"Gracias, amigo."*

"Es nada," the youngest victim of the hold up replied with a smile.

"G—God damn it!" Twelfinch ejaculated, believing he saw a way in which he could repay the lack of respect he had suffered at the hands of the Texan. Waving a finger which encompassed Martin, who was starting to rise ensuring both hands stayed well away from the butts of the guns, and the still sprawled out—although stirring—Dubs, he went on, "You assaulted peace officers in the execution of their duty!"

"There's some might call it that," Waco admitted, seeing hope come to the face of Martin at receiving such unexpected support.

"And there's some's might call it *exceeding* their duty," Glendon seconded. "Unless figuring on using a scatter on somebody for doing nothing more than saying Wyatt Harp's name's been made a crime."

"I don't consider it in that light!" the senator stated, although usually he would not have thought of taking such a supportive stand on the behalf of a peace officer.

"Every man's entitled to his opinion, 'cording to the Constitution of the good old U.S. of A.," the foreman admitted dryly. "Only I reckon *Major Mosehan'd* go along with me on mine."

"M—Major Mosehan?" Martin repeated, losing some of the satisfaction he had started to display.

"*Major Mosehan,*" Glendon reiterated. "He's sort of touchy when it comes to peace officers trying to abuse his hired help without *real* good cause."

"*His* hired help?" the deputy queried, looking from Waco to Franks and back.

"His hired help," the foreman lied, but with such conviction he might have been speaking the truth on oath. "Tex rides the rough string and Mr. Franks's the Hashknife outfit's book-keeper."

"That doesn't give them any right to attack officers of the law," Twelfinch objected, puzzled by the deputy who was no longer showing pleasure over his intervention.

"Seeing as they are 'officers of the law' is why I just took the scatter away from him, 'stead of throwing lead," Waco explained, wondering why the stocky man had interceded and intrigued by hearing what he knew to be a Brooklyn accent coming from one whose attire was that of a cowhand. Nodding to where Dubs was rising and still looking dazed, he continued, "And that other 'officer of the law,' as *you* call them, can count himself lucky Jed Franks jumped him. If he'd've been let go on with drawing on me, I was too far off to have stopped him with my bare hands, so I wouldn't've even *tried*."

"There's no call for *anybody* to get all head down and horns hooking, Tex," Glendon remarked, hoping the blond would justify a belief in his intelligence and take the hint. "I haven't heard the deputy say's how he's wanting to toss you and Mr. Franks in the pokey over what's happened."

"How do you feel about it?" Waco inquired, his tone less of a question than a challenge, as he turned his gaze to Martin.

"I'm willing to let it drop," the deputy replied, trying to sound magnanimous. Seeing a way by which he might bring the matter to an end, he continued with an assumed briskness, "Time's wasting, though. We should be getting a posse together—!"

"You certainly should!" Twelfinch supported, his normal antipathy toward peace officers returning with the reminder of his financial loss during the hold up.

"It's a mite late in the day to go after them," Tract pointed out. "Night'll be down way afore you can get to where they hit us."

"Fact being, you can't go there at all," Waco supplemented, glancing with satisfaction at Twelfinch who he knew to be a prominent adherent of the "Eastern law wrangler" in the affair of the sheriff of Coconino County.

"Why not?" the politician demanded.

"Because the hold up was done over the county line," the Texan explained. "Which, the deputy here doesn't have no jurisdiction on the other side."

Even as Twelfinch was realizing that he had been hoist on his own petard and others were deriving enjoyment from reaching a similar conclusion, there was an interruption.

Having made it to his feet Dubs had stood swaying during the latter stage of the conversation, then his eyes came to rest upon Franks.

"You god-damned bastard!" the deputy bellowed, once again starting to snatch at his holstered revolvers.

Chapter 8

SCARED CLOSE TO WHITE HAIRED

~~~~~~~

FOR ONCE IN HIS EVENTFUL YOUNG LIFE, WACO WAS taken by surprise as Deputy Sheriff Alfred "Leftie Alf" Dubs began to throw down on Jedroe Franks!

Nor, on this occasion, was the youngest victim of the hold up as prepared to cope with the situation as he had been when the peace officer tried to avenge what was happening to Deputy Sheriff Jackson Martin!

It would have gone badly for Franks if William "Fast Billy" Cromaty had really been as lacking in perception and slow moving as he generally conveyed the impression that he was!

Knowing the vicious and bullying nature of the deputy, the lanky cowhand had felt sure he would not allow the rough and humiliating treatment at Franks' hands to pass without reprisals. Therefore, while the conversation was taking place, he had moved unnoticed away from Peter Glendon's side. Passing through the crowd with the ease of an eel slipping out of the hands of a fisherman, he had come to a halt close to where Dubs was lying.

Stepping forward as the deputy yelled and sent both hands in the opening movements of a draw, Cromaty did not offer to duplicate the action as a means of ending it. Instead, he swung up his right foot. Seeming to expand like a set of lazy-tongs, his leg directed the sole of its boot on to the seat of Dubs' trousers. The power possessed by his apparently skeletal frame was demonstrated as he delivered more of a push than a kick.

Feeling himself suddenly assailed with considerable force from behind, Dubs let out a startled yell. Hands missing their objectives, he was powerless to prevent the unexpected thrust propelling him toward his intended victim. Or to avoid the response his behavior aroused. Coming around with a precision equal to that shown when tackling the deputy earlier, the punch thrown by Franks met his jaw as he came into range. Spun away, he once more went down. This time, he landed with his face on the ground and lay without a movement.

"Whooee!" Franks ejaculated, shaking his hand and working its fingers. "Now I know why that woman used a knuckle-duster!"

"Well now, senator," Waco drawled, allowing his half drawn Colts to return to their holsters. "Would *you* call that assaulting an officer of the law in the execution of his duty?"

"Or, seeing's how Mr. Franks isn't armed," Glendon supplemented, despite knowing this was not the case, as he too was returning the Remington he had been drawing. "Was it sort of exceeding his duty again, would you say."

"He is so armed!" protested Senator Paul Michael Twelfinch II. "There's a revolver under his jacket!"

"Is there, by grab?" the foreman gasped in what seemed to be surprise, despite having detected the slight bulge on the left side of the jacket and deducing its wearer was armed. "Looks like Fast Billy there couldn't've knowed about that."

"I for sure didn't," Cromaty asserted, with no greater veracity as he had been equally observant. However, having reverted to his usual appearance of vacant apathy, it was impossible for anybody who did not know him to believe he could be capable of guile as he went on dolefully, "Which same's why I cut in. I didn't want Mr. Dubs to get his-self hanged for shooting down an unarmed man."

"Now there's a right obliging gent, or I've *never* crossed one's trail!" Waco declared. "Folks hereabouts must admire their peace officers a whole heap to think so much about them. What do you say, deputy?"

"Help Alf back to the office some of you!" Martin

ordered, glaring around and declining to comment as he knew the lanky cowhand too well to be misled by the look of apparent simplicity. Waving a hand toward the tarpaulin wrapped corpse, he continued as he had twice already that day, "And some of you tote that body down to the undertaker's parlor!"

"Aren't you going to take a look at him?" Waco drawled.

"Is there any reason why I should—do it right now?" Martin asked, the last four words clearly an after-thought as the idea had never occurred to him.

"He's got him a real fine head of black hair, considering his eyes're blue," the blond answered, having been attracted by that point while helping prepare the body for transporting on the roof of the stagecoach. "It looks so real, you wouldn't hardly know it's a wig."

"A *wig*?" the deputy repeated, looking at Walter Tract. "Why would he be wearing a wig?"

"I didn't know he was," the driver admitted.

"Like I said, it's a real good one," Waco pointed out. "Some fellers wear one because they're bald, or going that way. Others do it to make them look different. Which same's why I got to wondering about him."

"Who is he?" Martin demanded of the driver.

"Said his name was 'Maurice Blenheim,' " Tract supplied. "I figured him to be a drummer of some sort, only they usually tell you what they're selling and he was travelling some too light to be toting samples."

"Was toting two hide-out guns, though, and, way you told it, must have reckoned himself snake enough to use them so fast he could stop himself getting killed when he fetched out the first," the blond drawled, that fact having added to his curiosity. "I know it's none of my never-mind, but I'd say he's a man who could stand some cutting on his sign back to where he came from."

"Let's get Alf and the body taken away!" Martin commanded, without offering to commit himself to following the advice.

"Are you going any farther today, driver?" Pierre Henri Jaqfaye inquired, breaking a silence which had endured since leaving the stagecoach.

"Nope," Tract answered. "We'll pull out at seven o'clock in the morning. You go along with the agent and he'll get you rooms at the Pima County Hotel."

"Haven't got 'round to trading names yet, friend," Waco remarked to Glendon, as the group began to go its various ways.

"Name's Glendon, Pete for short," the foreman supplied.

"They call me 'Waco,' " the blond drawled. "Only it's the OD Connected I ride for, not the Hashknife—Which I reckon you know part of."

"Reckoned letting on you and Mr. Franks there rode for Major Mosehan might make that knobhead john law a mite more friendly toward you," Glendon explained, nodding to where the young man was departing with the local agent of the Arizona State

Stage line and other two passengers. Turning his gaze back to the Texan, he went on hopefully, "Did you say you ride, or used to ride, for the OD Connected?"

"I'm still on the payroll," Waco replied. "And we'll be headed back there as soon as we've 'tended to something hereabouts."

"We?" the foreman hinted.

"Doc Leroy and me," the blond elaborated, then looked past Glendon. "Talk of the devil, here he comes now."

"Haven't you 'tended to our hosses yet?" demanded the pallid faced cowhand, strolling up.

"Got sort of kept busy," Waco replied. "How's the guard?"

"He'll come through," Doc said, showing relief to eyes which knew him well. "The doctor goes along with me that his skull isn't fractured."

What the slender Texan did not say was that, in addition to having had his diagnosis confirmed by a qualified medical practitioner, he had also been praised for the excellent work he had performed and making all the correct decisions.

"Do not worry, *m'sieur,*" Pierre Henri Jaqfaye instructed, a note of asperity coming into his voice as he held it at a low pitch. "I promised you that we will refund all the money you had stolen."

"And so you *should*!" Senator Paul Michael Twelfinch II claimed, the whining timbre of his words striking the Frenchman as irritating in the extreme. "If it hadn't been for you people, I wouldn't have been on the stagecoach to be robbed."

"I don't think anybody else in here is interested in that," Jaqfaye said coldly, the voice of the politician having risen as he was speaking. "Or perhaps the *wrong* people may be."

Having been allocated rooms at the Pima County Hotel by the depot agent of the Arizona State Stage Line, the two men were taking an evening meal in the dining room. They had not come in together. In fact, having had all he wanted of Twelfinch's company, Jaqfaye would have preferred to eat alone. He was given no choice in the matter. Entering as he was finishing a plate of apple pie, the politician had joined him at the table without so much as asking if doing so was all right.

"Don't forget how much I stand to lose by helping you!" Twelfinch whined, but in a lower and more discrete fashion. "After all, supporting your lawyer in that Coconino County business could have an adverse effect upon my political career."

"We appreciate what you are doing for us, *M'sieur le* Senator," the Frenchman asserted, although he was thinking, "Not anywhere nearly so adverse as the effect will be if you do *anything* that goes against *our* interests."

"You have to get my pocketbook back," Twelfinch stated.

"Why?"

"Because I've listed the names of all your people in it!"

"You've done *what*?" Jaqfaye hissed and, at that moment, he looked far from prissy or effeminate.

"It is for my *protection*!" Twelfinch explained, alarmed by the savagery with which the Frenchman was glaring at him. "Everything is written in shorthand, so *they* won't be able to read it, but it might fall into the hands of somebody who can."

"So it might!" Jaqfaye agreed.

"Anyway, your people shouldn't have any trouble in finding that Starr woman and her gang."

"Probably not, providing it was her and her gang."

"You don't believe that young fool, Franks, and the Texan, do you?"

"I'm keeping an open mind on it."

"Franks hasn't been in the West long enough to know what he's talking about," Twelfinch estimated. "And the Texan claimed to know her, which means he would try to make us believe she wasn't involved. All those god-damned Johnny Rebs stick together."

"That is as may be," the Frenchman answered, picking up the walking stick which was leaning on the table and pushing back his chair. "Anyway, as there is nothing I can do about it tonight and we have an early start in the morning, I am going to bed."

"Shall I come up to your room so we can—talk?" Twelfinch inquired archly.

"I'm *much* too tired for that," Jaqfaye refused, standing up. "Goodnight, *m'sieur*."

Turning, the Frenchman strode swiftly across the dining room. On entering the lobby, he glanced over his shoulder. Having satisfied himself that he was not being watched by Twelfinch, he made no attempt to go upstairs. Instead, muttering a Gallic profanity over not having brought his hat with him—although it had seemed unnecessary when all he had meant to do was have a meal before retiring for the night—he walked toward the front entrance.

During the latter part of the conversation, Jaqfaye had had the feeling that somebody was looking at him. Glancing around, he had discovered this to be the case. A tallish, well built, swarthily handsome, dark haired man was standing in the doorway connecting the dining room to the lobby. He had on the attire of a successful professional gambler and the ivory handle of a Colt Storekeeper Model Peacemaker in a cross-draw holster showed from beneath the left side of his black cutaway jacket. Seeing he had been noticed, he had given a jerking motion with his head in the direction of the front entrance. Then, donning the low crowned, wide brimmed black hat he was holding, he had swung around to depart the way he had indicated.

Despite having come out in response to the signal he received and seeing its maker standing on the sidewalk at the end of the building, Jaqfaye neither spoke nor went to join him. In fact, as soon as the Frenchman appeared, he started to walk in a leisurely appearing fashion across the plaza. Following him,

Jaqfaye made no attempt to catch up for some time. At last, having led the way through a less affluent part of the town, they were approaching a large house standing some distance from the nearest other buildings. It was well lit and emitted the sound of music, male and female voices raised in song, laughter and other indications of merry-making in progress.

"Well, *M'sieur* Atkinson?" Jaqfaye asked and, regardless of the impression of hardness conveyed by the gambler, his attitude was that of one who was addressing a social inferior.

"It's Madden, Mr. Jaqfaye," Norman Atkinson replied, showing none of the resentment which might have been expected of him when subjected to such behavior by the effeminate looking Frenchman, his voice that of a Southron.

"Is he drunk in there?" Jaqfaye demanded, knowing by the red light hanging on the porch that the building was a brothel.

"He's in there, or at least in one of the cabins Glory Joyce has out back," the gambler answered. "But he's not *drunk*."

"Then what is wrong with him?"

"He's scared close to white haired."

"Over what?"

"I'll let him tell you himself."

Setting off as he was speaking, Atkinson guided Jaqfaye around the building. Going to one of the half dozen small adobe *jacales* in a row a short distance behind it, he knocked with what was obviously a pre-arranged sequence. The lock clicked, a bolt was operated and the door opened. Only a trifle at first, then wider after the two men had been studied for a moment through the crack. Allowing them to enter without showing himself, the solitary occupant closed the door behind them as soon as they were inside.

Although no light had showed through the shutters covering the windows, the only room of the *jacale* was illuminated by a lamp hanging from the center of its ceiling. It was simply furnished with a comfortable looking bed, a dressing table, a small folding table and two chairs. Behind curtains in one corner was a commode for use by the occupants, but there were no other toilet facilities.

"Well, *M'sieur* Madden," the Frenchman greeted, in a far from friendly or encouraging fashion. "And what in the name of *le bon Diable* are you up to?"

"I've got to get away!" replied the frightened looking clerk, in a mixture of defiance and alarm. "Mosehan suspects me of being responsible for the attempts to kill him this afternoon!"

"I suppose that was inevitable," the Frenchman sighed. "*M'sieur* Mosehan is a *very* intelligent man, otherwise the Governor would not have selected him—Nor would we have considered it was imperative that he should not even discover what was wanted from him."

"It wasn't *my* fault he got as far as he did!" Atkinson stated, meeting the accusatory glances being directed his way by the other two men. It was apparent as he went on that he was addressing Jaqfaye, "I wanted to take him out myself somewhere before he got this far, but you said it was too risky and had to be done when he arrived. It wasn't easy picking up an even halfway good gun hand in this god-damned, one-hoss town."

"The two you did get weren't any use!" Madden accused.

"Witchet had enough guts to stay on and try again," the gambler pointed out coldly. Then, once again, he directed his next words to the Frenchman, "I told him to come here and hide out and said he'd gone out of town the other way when that damned knobhead deputy asked me if I'd seen him. I figured to have him cut Mosehan down in his room at the hotel, but this yahoo came to tell me he was sitting by the window in the bar and Witchety reckoned to take him out right there."

"And missed!" the clerk spat out.

"How could he, or anybody else, figure a god-damned cowhand fooling around would get shoved into the line of fire just as he touched off the shot?" Atkinson challenged.

"It was unfortunate," Jaqfaye supported.

"*Unfortunate?*" Madden almost screeched. "I'd say it was more than just 'mother-something' unfortunate. Mosehan knows he was the target and not the cowhand. When I got back to my room in the Governor's suite, luckily without them knowing I'd come, I heard him saying so. Then he started asking questions about *me*."

"Such as?" the Frenchman inquired.

"How long I'd been with the Governor and did I know why he'd been sent for and where the meeting was to take place."

"But did he say he suspected you?"

"Not while I was listening," Madden admitted. "Which wasn't long. As soon as I saw the way he was thinking, I got out as quietly as I'd got in and went to Atkinson."

"I'd told him where to find me," the gambler explained. "And, when I saw he was running scared, I figured I'd best stash him away. He wouldn't come here until I promised I'd fetch you to talk to him."

"Will he be safe *here*?" the Frenchman wanted to know.

"Sure," Atkinson declared with complete assurance. "Only Glory Joyce knows he's here and I've got enough on her to have her stretching hemp, so she won't talk."

"I'm not staying here!" Madden stated, glaring around the room with distaste.

"You will have to—!" Jaqfaye began.

"Like hell I will!" the clerk refused heatedly. "Either you get me out of Arizona with enough money to live in comfort for the rest of my life, or I'm going to Mosehan and tell him all I know!"

"Are you?" the Frenchman asked.

"I am, by god!" Madden affirmed, turning and hurrying toward the door. "And I'm going right now, unless you say you'll do everything I want!"

Chapter 9

I WANT TO MEET BELLE STARR

"IT'S NO USE, MAJOR," PETER GLENDON SAID, IN A mixture of bitterness and puzzlement, having arrived at the Pima County Hotel a couple of minutes too late to see Pierre Henri Jaqfaye leaving, and then sending a message asking the man he was addressing to join him in the bar room. "We haven't come across hide nor hair of Madden."

"He couldn't've hid his sign better even should he've sprouted wings and headed south like a swallow comes cold weather," supplemented William "Fast Billy" Cromaty, looking his most vacantly dim-witted. "But, was I to get asked, going by the way he's all of a suddenly not 'round any more, I'd say there *could* be something in you concluding's how it might've been him's pointed the way to have you made wolf bait both times it was tried."

"Just *could* be?" Major Bertram Mosehan asked dryly.

"Well now, sir," the lanky cowhand answered, blinking like a particularly unintelligent screech owl caught out in the bright sunlight. "My mammy allus told me's I shouldn't *never* say nothing was *certain* unless I'm right sure myself it is and, being *me,* not even then."

"If I could get the rights of it," the major informed the foreman. "That *might* make right good sense."

Taking into account having seen Erroll Madden looking at him as he was sitting by the window in the bar room, shortly before the shooting which had cost the life of an innocent passer-by, Mosehan had added it to his thoughts regarding the previous attempt on his life. Therefore, he had questioned the Governor of Arizona about the clerk. Although he had learned nothing to satisfy his curiosity, his suppositions had been strengthened when he was told by the bellboy on duty at the reception desk in the lobby of Madden's arrival and hurried departure while he was conversing with "Mr. Jervis."

On Glendon and Cromaty having come to report, the major had told them of his belief that Madden had betrayed him to his intended killers on both occasions. Without being in any way sycophantic, they had expressed agreement with his point of view. After he had had described all that had taken place behind the depot of the Arizona State Stage Line, he had asked them to go in search of Madden. Neither thought of questioning the order, which was how each regarded it despite the polite way it had been worded. They were aware of why he had delegated the task to them. Not only did they know the town of Marana and its population far better, but he had matters with "Mr. Jervis" demanding his attention.

Unfortunately, although they had performed the search adequately within the limits of the knowledge they had at their disposal, the efforts of the two men had been without success!

"I'm damned if I can figure out where he went," Glendon declared. "He came in on the Governor's private coach and it's still here. Unless he's gone on foot, which I wouldn't reckon's likely, he must still be somewhere around town. He hasn't hired a horse, or a rig, from the livery barn and, so far as we've heard, nobody's found out he's widelooped one or the other from them."

"He doesn't know anybody who lives here," Mosehan remarked. "At least, the Governor says he's never mentioned anybody and reckoned he'd never been here when they were coming up from Phoenix and, before anybody tells me, I know that's what he would say under the circumstances even if he'd been born and raised here."

"Which he wasn't," Cromaty drawled. "Maybe those two gunnies had somebody else in on the deal with them, maj'. That same company, seeing's how they didn't come through it alive, could've concluded it'd be safer for all concerned was Madden to be took off out of town and had hosses, or a rig, it could be done on."

"It's possible," Mosehan admitted, not in the least surprised by this latest example of the reasoning power possessed by the lanky cowhand. "Which brings up something else that's puzzling me."

"Who's trying to get you killed," Glendon guessed.

"Way I see it, which's likely all wrong," Cromaty said soberly. "It's somebody who don't want you to take on this chore for the Governor, maj'. Or somebody's is hoping we'll figure that's the way the trail runs."

"You figure somebody with a grudge might figure this chore for the Governor makes a good chance of covering their sign, should the major have wound up dead?"

"That's how it could be, Pete."

"If it's the last, I can't for the life of me think who the son-of-a-bitch doing it might be!" Mosehan claimed. "Hell, I know I've made my share of enemies, but I can't bring to mind any one of them who would have been able to learn what was doing with the Governor. Or, rather, when and where the meeting was to take place."

"He could've got *that* from Madden," the foreman pointed out.

"Sure," the major admitted. "But I still can't think who it could be."

"Then maybe we should try cutting the sign for somebody's doesn't want you taking on the chore," Cromaty suggested. "I'd reckon, 'specially should that Eastern law twister gets his wantings up to Coconino County, there'd be a whole slew of owlhoots around who wouldn't want no company of peace officers who could come and go anywhere over county lines."

"That's true enough," Mosehan agreed. "But, apart from Curly Bill Brocius and Johnny Ringo,[1] I can't think of any of them who would be smart enough, or have the kind of connections, to arrange things the way they happened."

"Curly and Johnny are slick enough," Glendon accepted, but with reservations. "Only I don't reckon neither of them would *hire* to get you killed."

"If they did," the lanky cowhand added. "They'd've picked somebody a whole heap better than those two yahoos we put down."

"That's the way I see it," the major said grimly, having met the two men in question and formed a surprisingly favorable opinion of their character if not their honesty. "Well, sitting here talking isn't going to give us the answers."

"There's only one feller who can," Glendon asserted. "And that's Madden his-self."

---

1. The outlaws, Johnny Ringo and Curly Bill Brocius make "guest" appearances respectively in: *Case Four, "Jase Holmes' Killer,"* and *Case Five, "Statute Of Limitations," SAGEBRUSH SLEUTH*. The latter also "guests" in: *Chapter Two, "The Juggler And The Lady"* and *Chapter Three, "The Petition," WACO RIDES IN* and in *Part Six, "Keep Good Temper Alive," J.T.'S HUNDREDTH.* J.T.E.

"Trouble being, we can't find him," Cromaty went on dolefully. " 'Course, we *might* get *real* lucky and have him come looking for us, all ready to tell what's doing."

Before either Mosehan or Glendon could make any answer, there was a distraction in the form of revolver shots!

"Very well, *m'sieur,*" Pierre Henri Jaqfaye said, sounding almost on the verge of breaking into tears and reaching with his left hand to prevent Norman Atkinson drawing the Colt Storekeeper Model Peacemaker from its holster. "You are leaving us without any alternative."

"I thought you'd see it *my* way!" Erroll Madden declared, but without releasing his hold on the latch of the door or looking around.

"As I said, you have left me with no other choice, *mon ami,*" the Frenchman sighed. "I will give you what you *deserve.*"

Although the disloyal clerk had started to experience serious qualms as he was crossing the room, realizing that having walked away from a man he knew to be a hired killer—the dress style of a professional gambler notwithstanding—after delivering such an ultimatum might be most ill-advised, he had taken comfort from the belief that he was safe in doing so. In his estimation, Atkinson would not chance firing a revolver with so many people at the brothel who were sure to hear the shot. Nor, he had told himself, would the gambler dare to harm a person with his important connections in the capital of Arizona.

There were serious flaws in both suppositions, but Madden had failed to take them into consideration!

Hearing what was being said by Jaqfaye, who he regarded as posing no threat whatsoever to his well being, a surge of elation rose and the clerk was satisfied that he had won his demands!

Turning with a smugly triumphant smirk, Madden was enjoying an unusual sensation of power. It was created by an assumption that, for once in his life, he was in a position from which he could control events. Such a thing had never happened before and he intended to make the most of it. He wondered how much money he should demand as the price of his silence.

The satisfaction and speculation ended almost immediately!

Taking the restraining hand from the sleeve of the gambler, Jaqfaye had transferred it to join the other in grasping the shining black walking stick. As he was going toward the clerk with a swift and almost balletic grace, which was charged with deadly menace in spite of the somewhat effeminate movements, he tugged in opposite directions. Liberated and sliding from the wooden outer sheath, the blade of what was clearly a sword came into view. While slender, it was shaped like an *épée de combat* and he was handling it in the fashion of one.

Unlike a fencing foil, which it also resembled, such a weapon could be used to cut as well as thrust!

Wielded with the skill of a master swordsman, glinting briefly in the light of the lamp suspended from the center of the ceiling, the blade flickered around almost too rapidly for the human eye to follow. Sharp as a razor, the cutting edge passed beneath Madden's chin and laid open his throat to the bone before he could utter a sound. As he stumbled involuntarily backward against the door, blood gushing redly from a mortal wound, his assailant struck again. Going into a classic lunge, the Frenchman directed the point to impale his heart and withdrew it when its unnecessary task was done.

"As I said, *m'sieur!*" Jaqfaye purred almost disinterestedly, watching the lifeless body sliding to the floor. "Just what you deserve!"

"The god-damned stupid son-of-a-bitch!" Atkinson growled, showing no surprise over the speed and murderous efficiency displayed by the Frenchman. "As if we'd just stand back and let him walk out of here after what he said."

"It wasn't the most sensible thing he could have said, or done," Jaqfaye seconded and bent to wipe clean the bloody blade on the clothing of his victim.

"I'll clean things up here and get rid of him," the gambler offered, waving a hand toward the body and the blood which ran on to the floor from the wound in the throat. "It'd be best for all concerned that Glory Joyce doesn't find out what happened."

"I leave it in your hands, *m'sieur,*" the Frenchman

accepted. "And I know I can rely upon you to ensure his body will not be found."

"Sure," Atkinson grunted, knowing the other too well to show any resentment over being reminded of something so basic.

"There is another matter, *mon ami*," Jaqfaye warned.

"God damn it!" the gambler ejaculated furiously, after he had been told about the hold up of the stagecoach and theft of the incriminating pocketbook from Senator Paul Michael Twelfinch II. "And I called *Madden* stupid!"

"I know what you mean!" the Frenchman admitted in a vicious hiss. "It is a great pity that I cannot treat *le bon* Senator in the same manner. Unfortunately, we still have use for him."

"That's the way it goes," Atkinson drawled, more philosophically.

"True," Jaqfaye conceded, also reverting to his more normal tone. "But we still have to get the pocketbook back to make sure it doesn't fall into the wrong hands."

"Like *his*?"

"His, more than anybody else's."

"Thing being, who do I have to pass the word to look for?"

"It seems the hold up may have been carried out by Belle Starr and her gang."

"Does it, by god?" Atkinson demanded.

"It *seems* she was responsible," the Frenchman

corrected. "However, one of the other passengers doesn't think this is the case and he has put up sound arguments to support his view."

"Who is he?"

"A young man called 'Franks.' "

"Is he a peace officer?"

"Not that he mentioned," Jaqfaye replied. "And, if he should be, I would say he is from the East and not a Westerner."

"A dude, huh?" the gambler asked.

"Possibly *you* would regard him as a dude," the Frenchman answered and described the doubts and suppositions expressed by the youngest surviving passenger.

"Like you say, he's got some right good thoughts on it," Atkinson conceded, at the conclusion of the explanation. "Only, going by all I've heard of her, she's smart enough to have been pulling a *double* bluff."

"A *double* bluff?" Jaqfaye repeated, examining the blade fastidiously and, satisfied all traces of blood were removed, returning it to the wooden sheath in which it had been concealed until required for use. "You mean that she and her men made the apparently unintentional and indiscrete comments so it would appear they were only pretending to be themselves?"

"It could be," the gambler affirmed. "What I can't figure out is why they'd go to all that trouble to hold up a stagecoach. For Belle Starr to be interested, there'd have to be a fair slew of money involved. Was it carrying plenty in the strongbox?"

"Not that I know of. At least, they never even asked about it, much less had it down to look. However, the man they killed was apparently carrying a large sum they knew about. It could have been him, rather than the strongbox, they were after and the rest of us were just incidental to him."

"That could be, too."

"The thing is, *mon ami*," Jaqfaye said pensively. "Were we robbed by Belle Starr and her gang?"

"I dunno," Atkinson replied. "But she's in Arizona."

"You are sure of that?" the Frenchman asked.

"Feller I got it from knows her from up in the Indian Nations," the gambler explained. "Way he told it, she was making her way down to Tucson, but he didn't know what she's up to."

"Could you find out whether she is there, please?" Jaqfaye requested. "No matter whether it was she and her gang who robbed the stagecoach or not, I want to meet Belle Starr!"

Seated at the sidepiece which served as a writing and dressing-table, Jedroe Franks was distracted from the letter he was writing by hearing the door of his room opening!

Yet the young man had turned the key in the lock on entering!

As was the case with the other two passengers, Franks had been found accommodation for the night

at the Pima County Hotel. After they were assigned
to their temporary quarters, Pierre Henri Jaqfaye had
arranged with the depot agent of the Arizona State
Stage Line for a sum equivalent to that stolen from
the young man to be made available to him. Although necessity had demanded he accept, with the
proviso that it was a loan given on his note of hand
and not a gift, he had had no desire to extend his acquaintance with the Frenchman or Senator Paul
Michael Twelfinch II. Nor, even if he had had an ul-
terior motive for his generosity, had Jaqfaye showed
any inclination to do so.

Having eaten alone, Franks returned to his room.
He was not tired, nor did he feel like going in search
of some form of diversion. Instead, he had settled
down and started to write a letter to his home in
Hartford, Connecticut. Much as he hated to do so, he
intended to ask for money. The necessity angered
him, for he knew his widowed mother was far from
wealthy. However, he was even less enamored of the
prospect of remaining obligated to the Frenchman.

The disinclination to be placed in such a situation,
in case there might be an attempt to exploit it sexually instead of by a repayment of the money, was only
one reason for the young man having decided to try
to locate and bring to justice the gang who had
robbed him!

However, the idea of doing so was neither as fool-
hardy or impractical as it might appear on the surface!

Franks might have only recently arrived in Arizona Territory and had not been for any extensive period west of the Mississippi River, but he was far from being a helpless "dude" where matters of survival were concerned!

Although his vision at long distances was sufficiently poor to necessitate the use of spectacles, which he did not require for such things as reading and writing, the young man had always led an active life. As a boy growing up in the farming country around his home town, he had been encouraged to participate in a variety of healthy outdoor activities. Hunting and camping expeditions away from the more civilized areas of Connecticut had taught him lessons in survival which he had never forgotten or let fall into disuse. What was more, on going to college, he had engaged upon boxing, wrestling and other sports to keep him physically fit.

Always interested in the enforcement of law and order, but disinclined to follow his father into the legal and courtroom side, Franks had nevertheless devoted much time to studies designed to help him enter the practical side in that field. He had concluded the West offered greater opportunities than his home area, or any of the larger Eastern cities, for finding the kind of employment as a peace officer he desired. Unfortunately, the uncle he had travelled to meet in Tucson and who had promised to help him achieve his ambition had died three days before he arrived. In spite of that, never one to give up without a struggle in the face of difficulties, he had been travelling to Phoenix to try to obtain an appointment in a law enforcement agency by his own efforts.

Even without his reservations over the loan from Jaqfaye, therefore, the young man would have been determined to make an attempt to recover his property!

In addition to the hold up of the stagecoach having deprived Franks of all the money he had with him, the carpetbag had held items which had great personal importance and significance for him. He came from a sturdy stock which did not turn the other cheek when they were subjected to any form of hostile treatment. What was more, he realized that—due to the conditions prevailing currently in Arizona Territory, as a result of the incident affecting the sheriff of Coconino County—the local peace officers were likely to be restricted in their efforts to locate and apprehend the gang. Being a free agent, he considered he was better able to conduct a search for them. If he should be successful, unless he had the opportunity to make a citizen's arrest of the gang—which he had concluded was unlikely—he would be able to lead the appropriate local peace officers to help capture them.

These were the conclusions drawn by the young man!

It was Franks' intention to put them into effect the following morning instead of continuing the journey by stagecoach to Phoenix!

Reaching instinctively for his spectacles as he heard the door being opened, the young man looked over his shoulder. Somewhat restricted though his vision might be without them, he could see sufficiently well to be warned there was nothing as harmless involved as somebody having entered his room by accident. Nor was it a member of the hotel staff coming in for some legitimate, if unannounced, purpose. Even in the unlikely event of two locks receiving identical keys, at least as far as those allocated to the guests were concerned, the person who was stepping across the threshold would not have been carrying a cocked revolver, or any other kind of weapon.

What was more, there was a further indication that the intentions of the newcomer were far from innocent!

Tallish, lean, and clad in old, well worn clothing of cowhand style, his twin holstered gunbelt carrying the walnut handled mate to the Colt Civilian Model Peacemaker he was holding, the intruder had covered his head by a hood made from a flour sack with holes for the eyes cut in it!

Finding himself observed by the occupant of the room, the newcomer gave vent to a muffled profanity and, with closer to a jerk than a smoothly flowing swing, brought forward the Colt until its barrel reached waist level and aligned instinctively. On arriving there, a snatch at the trigger released the hammer. Freed from restrain, it snapped forward to play its part in the firing process.

Chapter 10

YOU DIDN'T DO THE "GOODNIGHTING"

TWO THINGS SAVED THE LIFE OF JEDROE FRANKS as the Colt Civilian Peacemaker was fired at him!

The method employed by the masked intruder, also the skill displayed, was not conducive to great accuracy!

Furthermore, the young man responded to the threat with commendable rapidity!

Rising in a twisting motion which sent the chair skidding away, Franks flung himself across the room in a plunging dive. He moved so quickly that, although the margin was only small, he evaded the bullet which was directed at him. What was more, before he alighted on hands and knees, he had contrived to slip on the spectacles picked up when hearing the door being opened. Making no attempt to rise, he scuttled across the floor on all fours toward the bed. Not only was he seeking shelter behind it, he wanted to retrieve the Colt Storekeeper Model Peacemaker from the spring retention shoulder holster he had hung on the back of a chair by its head.

Twice more the revolver bellowed before the young man reached the bed, but the intruder was no more fortunate than on the first attempt to shoot him. Hearing the lead striking the floor close behind him, it gave an added inducement to rapid movement. Then, seeing the thickness of the mattress and hanging covers alongside him, he prepared to arm himself. Indicative of his cool assessment of the situation in the face of considerable danger, he was too wise to rise and present a target. Instead, tipping over the chair with his left hand, he grabbed the butt of the short barrelled revolver in his right. As he was doing so, he heard indications that the intruder was moving.

Looking under the bed, Franks discovered that the hooded visitor had turned and was leaving the room. Not merely departing, however, but closing the door in passing. Wrenching the Colt from the spring clips of the holster, he rose swiftly with the intention of following. However, common sense overcame the desire induced by anger to dash out recklessly in an attempt to obtain revenge for the attempt upon his life, instead, he behaved in a manner so sensible it would have met the approval of an experienced Western peace officer and gun fighter.

On reaching the door, Franks stood to the side and eased it open. As he was doing so, he ascertained how the intruder had gained admittance. Although he had not heard it land, his key had been shoved out of the hole from the other side. In its place, he noticed, was another he suspected to be one of the "masters" by which employees of the hotel were granted access to any room.

No shots were fired as the door opened!

Wasting no time in wondering how the intruder had come into possession of the master key, Franks peered cautiously from his room!

The hooded visitor had not waited to deal with any pursuit which was attempted!

Having run along the corridor immediately on leaving, the intruder was already on the point of quitting the hotel. As was generally the case in such establishments, ropes were supplied by the windows on the upper floor to serve as escapes in case of fire. Clearly having made preparations for a hurried departure, he was already seated across the sill of the open window at the end—which overlooked the alley separating the building from its neighbor—and on the point of returning the Colt to its holster so he could grasp the rope.

"Halt!" Franks yelled, stepping from the room and adopting the sideways to the objective, arms' length and shoulder height stance of a target shooter or a duellist.

Once again the intruder fired!

Ignoring the bullet which hissed by to break the window at the other end of the corridor, the young man responded in kind!

Although he came close to making a hit, Franks' accuracy was no greater than that of his attacker!

For all that, the young man had no cause to feel he had failed in his purpose!

Startled by the lead striking the frame of the window above his head, to sent splinters of wood pattering on to the flour sack hood, the intruder jerked backward involuntarily. Releasing the Peacemaker as he felt himself losing his balance, he was only partly successful in the use to which he put the liberated hand. While he prevented himself from toppling headlong into the alley, he slipped over the sill and dropped feet first to the ground.

"Agh!" Franks heard yelled by a voice filled with pain, in echo to something heavy landing in the alley below the window. "M—My leg! I've broken my leg, J—!"

The deep boom of a shotgun brought the words to an immediate halt!

Already running toward the window when the shouting commenced, the young man looked out. His gaze went first to where the intruder was sprawled supine, arms and legs extended in the haphazard way only death could achieve. Having done so, he looked next in the direction from which the shotgun had been fired. Even without noticing the faint glint reflected upon a badge of office, he would have identified the approaching figure as Deputy Sheriff Jackson Martin. However, at the sight of the shotgun's barrels being elevated toward his position, he pulled back his head without offering to announce who he was and his reason for being there.

The precaution proved advisable!

Giving another deep cough, the shotgun emitted its second charge of nine .32 caliber buckshot balls!

If Franks had remained peering out of the window, at least one of the released load would have hit him!

Footsteps were pounding up the stairs!

Turning, the young man was relieved by the sight of Major Bertram Mosehan leading those of the hotel employees and occupants of the bar room coming, guns in hand, to investigate the shooting!

"What's happening?" Mosehan inquired.

"A masked man broke into my room and started shooting when he found me there," Franks replied, wondering if he should tell of his suspicions regarding the reason for the visit. Deciding against doing so, he lowered the hammer and tucked the Storekeeper into his waist band. "He fell out of the window when I fired at him, then Deputy Martin shot him in the alley."

"It looks like he tried to hit him up here," the major commented, gazing at the furrow carved in the side of the window frame by the buckshot ball.

"That was aimed at me," Franks corrected.

"At *you*?" Mosehan repeated.

"He must have thought I was another intruder." the young man stated.

This was the explanation offered by Martin when Franks and the major went into the alley. The deputy was standing with William "Fast Billy" Cromaty and Peter Glendon, who had gone through the front entrance of the Pima County Hotel instead of accompanying Mosehan upstairs.

"Who is he?" Franks inquired, seeing the body had not been touched.

"Well I'll be damned!" Glendon ejaculated, staring at the face which he had revealed by removing the extemporized hood. "It's your bunkie, Martin!"

"Good god, so it is!" the peace officer admitted, also looking at the agony distorted features of Deputy Sheriff Alfred "Leftie Alf" Dubs. Making a gesture of annoyance, he continued, "I wondered why he asked me to stand his watch tonight. If I'd have realized—!"

"If you'd realized what?" Mosehan asked, as the words trailed away.

"I knew he was furious about the way this du—*Mr.* Franks had rough-handled and humiliated him," Martin explained. "But I never thought he would carry it to such extremes as to go to his room and try to kill him!"

"Well, yes sir," the man who had introduced himself as "Honest David Warburton" boomed, with either real or well assumed joviality. "I don't mind admitting that bull there isn't what you'd call yearling stock, which's why we're willing to let him go so reasonable priced. Isn't it, boys?"

"It sure is, Brother Dave," confirmed the member of the trio who had been presented by the speaker as, "Brother Matthew," and "Brother Luke" gave a similar concurrence in a voice just as indicative of coming from the Pacific Northwest coast country.

Studying the three men, Herbert Gilpin felt vaguely uneasy!

At five foot seven, with a stocky build suggestive of corpulence, there was now something oily and unctuous about the features of the eldest Warburton. Despite wearing the kind of clothing typical of a working cowhand, his sun-reddened features and bearing were reminiscent of a carnival "talented talker" seeking to persuade the passing "marks" they would receive good value for their money if they paid to enter his "ten-in-one."[1]

For all that, "Honest David" was far more prepossessing than the men he claimed to be his siblings.

While they were related, by the same father but different mothers, there was little family resemblance between the eldest and two younger Warburtons. Both were tall, gangling, lanky, unshaven and with hard features. They too were dressed like cowhands. However, while the elder's was equally worn, his garments showed signs of attention. Those they had on were dirty in the way of wearers who cared little for

---

1. "Ten-in-one": American carnival, fairground, term for a number of one or two person acts—such as sword swallowers, fire eaters, fortune tellers, Indian "fakirs," etc.—not necessarily just ten, who all appear in the same large marquee. J.T.E.

their personal appearance. An even more important difference set him apart from them. Each had a Colt Peacemaker in the tied-down holster of his gunbelt, but Honest David showed no sign of being armed.

Attracted by glowing accounts of the booming cattle industry in the West, Gilpin had sold his prosperous farm in New Hampshire and moved to Arizona Territory to try to accrue one of the vast fortunes he had frequently heard were being made. On his arrival, he had soon discovered the stories were greatly exaggerated. However, having studied the situation with care, he had concluded there was a possibility of making a better profit than was possible from the property he had left in the East. When selling him a small ranch on Burro Creek near Bagdad in Yavapai County, the previous owner had admitted frankly it required more stock. He had also suggested this could be obtained at the forthcoming sale of livestock to be held in Marana.

Travelling to the town ready for the appointed day, Gilpin had found his informant had been correct about the number of cattle and horses in particular which were available. What had not been taken into account was that the affair was, as a later generation would term such a situation, a "seller's market." In other words, so many potential purchasers were present, prices tended to be reflected in their willingness to buy.

Visiting the bar room of the Pima County Hotel where he was staying, with the intention of seeking solace for his disappointment, the rancher had been drawn into a conversation by Honest David. He had found nothing out of the ordinary, nor even unexpected, in the topic they had embarked upon. All around, men were discussing the prices being asked and paid for the livestock on offer. Even the three fatal shootings of the previous day, which would otherwise have been the main item of attention, were disregarded under the circumstances.

Learning that Gilpin had been unsuccessful in obtaining any stock, Honest David had offered a solution. He and his brothers, he had said, had speculated their wages on the purchase of a bull and twenty cows. As had been their intention in coming to Marana, they would be willing to part with the herd if made a reasonable offer. After the display of a bill of sale to establish legitimate ownership and the right to sell, the two men had indulged in a brief session of haggling. Soon, with the proviso that the sale would only take place if the animals met with the approval of the buyer, a price had been agreed upon. It was somewhat higher than Gilpin had intended paying, although just within his means, but less than any other figure he had been quoted.

On being told that the herd was being held in an area some distance from where the main sales were taking place, Gilpin had started to feel suspicious. However, saying frankly that he anticipated such an emotion even though it had not been expressed, Honest David had explained why the animals were not closer. His half-brothers could not be trusted to show restraint if able to obtain hard liquor and, furthermore, enemies they had made as a result of a drunken fracas were present. Wanting to avoid trouble, he had considered it advisable to keep them clear of temptation.

As evidence of his good will, on learning the rancher's two hands had disappeared on a spree earlier, the stocky man had offered to help bring in the cattle if they were acceptable. He had also suggested Gilpin placed all his money in the safe at the hotel before leaving to conduct the examination. When the rancher had said this was unnecessary, the red faced speculator had insisted he took the precaution. Then, as a further indication of his honorable intentions, Honest David had been adamant that Gilpin used the spare saddled horse he had with him. In this way, he had pointed out with disarming joviality, the rancher had nothing to lose by accompanying him.

During the whole of the something over two miles needed to reach their destination, the speculator had entertained the rancher with amusing anecdotes about various well known figures in the Territory. He had made himself so pleasant, Gilpin had experienced no qualms over the distance they were covering. Nor did the rancher have any fears for his safety when, having seen no other human beings for some time, they had passed through a clump of dense and extensive woodland to where the cattle were grazing on the banks of a stream in a clearing. Despite having had the two men who were present introduced as

"Brother Matthew" and "Brother Luke," he was not impressed by them. Looking at their surly faces, he could more readily accept the reason he had been given for the need to hold the animals so far from Marana. He could envisage each as a drunken rowdy of the kind likely to have made enemies eager to take revenge. For all that, as he had not brought any money or even his own horse and saddle with him, he took comfort from the realization that he had nothing worth stealing.

Clearly, regardless of the unsavory appearance presented by the younger Warburtons, the cattle had been made ready for the arrival of a potential buyer. They were of a kind Gilpin had seen in plenty since coming west of the Mississippi River. Resulting from generally inadvertant crosses between the longhorn variety—the use of which had paved the way for Texas to make an economic recovery after the consequences of supporting the Confederate States in the War of Secession[2]—and whitefaced Herefords brought in to replace them, such crosses possessed the good qualities of each parent. One of the traits acquired was to make them more tractable than the half wild, free ranging longhorns; specimens of which would have been exceptional hard to subject to the treatment accorded to the animals in the clearing. To render an examination easier, the fore and hind legs

---

2. How the means for economic recovery came into being is told in: *GOODNIGHT'S DREAM, FROM HIDE AND HORN* and *SET TEXAS BACK ON HER FEET.* J.T.E.

of each was secured by hobbles. As added security, the bull was fastened by a lariat around its neck to a sturdy bush.

Even without going close, Gilpin had seen that all the cattle were in good physical condition. However, while the cows were all young enough to meet with his approval, even a casual glance established the bull was of a much greater age.

Noticing the prospective buyer was looking with less than enthusiasm at the male animal, Honest David had made his comment and been supported by his half-brothers.

"I'll say it isn't a *yearling*," Gilpin replied, showing no sign of being impressed by the remarks. "And he hasn't been one for a *long* time. Damn it, Mr. Warburton, I told you I wanted a bull for breeding."

"This one's still good for that," Honest David asserted. "And, seeing's how it's been 'goodnighted,' it'll keep on being able to for some time to come."

" 'Goodnighted,' huh?" the rancher said, trying to prevent himself showing he was interested as he was aware what was implied by the term.

Discovered by the famous rancher and trail boss, Colonel Charles Goodnight,[3] the technique to which the men referred was a means to increase the period of sexual usefulness of a bull. The operation was per-

---

3. Colonel Charles Goodnight makes "guest" appearances in the three volumes referred to in *Footnote 2* above and in: *SIDEWINDER*. The military title was honorary, being granted as a tribute to his ability as a fighting man and leader. J.T.E.

formed by pushing the "seeds" of the testicles up against the belly and cutting off the entire unoccupied bag. With this done, the edges of the wound were sewed together, generally with strands unravelled from a piece of grass rope.

"It sure is," Honest David confirmed, waving a hand toward the secured animal. "You take a look. I did it so recent, the stitches are still in the cut."

"They're there, for sure," a voice with a Texas accent put in. "But *you* didn't do the 'goodnighting'!"

Startled exclamations burst from all the brothers as they and Gilpin looked in the direction from which the words were spoken. Although the younger pair started to reach toward the butts of their holstered Colts, Honest David gave a hurried order to, "Leave 'em be!" Unlike Matthew and Luke, or at least even more quickly, he had realized that—young though each undoubtedly was—the two Texas cowhands strolling in what appeared to be a leisurely fashion and empty handed from among the trees fringing the clearing were men with whom it would be extremely unwise to take chances.

"And just what's *that* supposed to mean?" the stocky man demanded, although he could have made a pretty accurate guess at what was portended by the remark.

"Like I said," Waco answered. "That old bull's been 'goodnighted' right recent, only *you* didn't do it."

"Hold hard there!" Gilpin requested, sensing a

threat to his intended purchase. "If you're saying these cattle don't belong to the gents here, I've seen a bill of sale for them."

"Well now," the blond countered. "That being, it should be signed by Colonel Raines, seeing's how they're all carrying his brand."

"Sure they're wearing his brand," Honest David admitted, pointing to two different marks of ownership—one of which having a "bar" line burned through it—borne by each animal. "But the feller we *bought* them off had put a 'vent' across it and slapped on his own."

"And, after you bought them all legal," Waco said quietly, "you figured that bull was too old to sell without and 'goodnighted' him?"

"That's just what I did," the stocky man affirmed, exuding an aura of honesty and truthfulness which was most convincing.

"Which being," the blond youngster drawled. "You won't have any objection to Doctor Gillespie from town coming on out here to take a look at how it's been stitched up?"

"Huh?" Honest David grunted, then saw a man clad in town dweller's clothes and carrying a black medical bag standing at the edge of the clearing. Reaching with his left hand, he started to scratch at his near side ribs and said, "God damn it, on top of everything else, I must've picked up a 'mother-something' flea!"

"Why should we need the doctor to look at it?"

Matthew challenged. "It ain't hurting none from the stitches."

"That's nothing to do with it, *hombre,*" the blond replied, but his next words were directed to the oldest of the Warburtons. "I haven't any notion how much *you* savvy about doctoring, mister, but whoever did the stitching on that old bull's bag sure knew plenty. Fact being, I reckon the doctor'll find out it's fastened with the kind of knots only a feller who knows doctoring real good can tie."

"Is that so?" asked Honest David, sounding almost disinterested, his hand continuing the scratching motions as it disappeared beneath the jacket he wore and behind his back.

"It's called a 'surgical purse string suture'," Doc Leroy elaborated, breaking the silence he had maintained since entering the clearing. "My daddy was a doctor. He taught me how to tie it and, 'though I'm usually most modest, I've got to say I've been told I can do it real good."

"Do tell," the stocky man answered, still without any discernible trace of rancor or growing interest.

Regardless of how the words sounded, there was nothing innocent about the way in which Honest David acted as he was saying them!

Having grasped the butt of the British made, short barrelled Webley Royal Irish Constabulary revolver in the holster attached almost horizontally to the back of his waist belt, the stocky man started to bring it out with the speed of a competent gun fighter.

Being aware of the manner in which their half-brother was armed and what had been potended by his apparently harmless scratching, the other two Warburtons once again began to grab for their weapons!

Chapter 11

YOU *ARE* BELLE STARR

ALTHOUGH NOTHING HAD SHOWN IN HIS EXPRESSION, voice and demeanor, a growing anger had assailed Honest David Warburton from the moment he had realized what must have brought the two Texas cowhands to the clearing!

Until the arrival of the pair, everything had been going as smoothly as the red faced cattle "speculator" could have desired!

To the best of Honest David's knowledge, the theft of the herd had not even been reported and no pursuit of himself and his half-brothers was taking place!

Making use of his well developed capability for judging character, the "speculator" had selected Herbert Gilpin as the most suitable candidate to purchase the stolen cattle. Clearly a comparative newcomer to the ranching business, he had seemed likely to accept the fake bill of sale. Furthermore, as following him for some time while he was seeking to buy stock legitimately had established, he was eager—even desperate—to purchase. Approached properly, including the precautions Honest David had suggested to ensure Gilpin's fears of being robbed were calmed when he had learned how far he would have to go to examine the animals, the selection had been justified.

However, the coming of the Texans and Doctor Gillespie threatened to put the whole scheme in jeopardy!

When he had noticed how neatly the wound on the "goodnighted" bull had been stitched, Honest David had concluded the operation had been performed by somebody with much greater skill and surgical knowledge than was possessed by the average cowhand. Remembering his supposition, he now began to make an accurate guess at the identity of the slender young Texan to whom the work was attributed.

Yet, regardless of suspecting with whom he and his half-brothers were in contention, the "speculator" believed the situation was not entirely hopeless!

Providing the two Texans and the doctor from Marana could be silenced, Gilpin might still be willing to buy the cattle and keep the matter to himself if it was pointed out that he would be considered an accomplice to the deed!

The problem was how to carry out the silencing!

There was, Honest David considered, a satisfactory solution!

Past experience had taught the "speculator" that being left handed had its advantages, one of which was that the trait was not immediately discernible to strangers!

Therefore, in the past, the production of the Webley Royal Irish Constabulary revolver from its place of concealment, using the near hand, had never failed to take victims by surprise!

Unfortunately for Honest David, while he was correct with regards to the identity of the Texans—Waco being as well known as Doc Leroy—there was one thing about them which he had failed to take into consideration!

The omission was one of ignorance, but had the effect of ruining a generally successful line of action!

Not only were the two young Texans experienced in all matters *pistolero,* they had spent much time in the company of the already legendary Rio Hondo gun wizard, Dusty Fog. Being aware of his completely ambidextrous prowess, neither ever discounted the possibility of an enemy possessing ability to use the left instead of the more general right hand.

Therefore, Waco and Doc were not caught unawares by the hitherto successful methods employed by the stocky "speculator"!

What was more, each was fully capable of dealing with the threats to their lives!

Swiftly though the blond moved to defend himself, his pallid featured companion proved even faster!

There was a white fluttering motion and the ivory handled Colt Civilian Model Peacemaker seemed to leap from the carefully designed holster to meet the right hand of its owner in midair. Raised into alignment with exceptional rapidity, flame erupted from the muzzle. Hit in the center of the chest, while his own weapon was still being turned forward, Honest David lost his grip on the butt as he was twisted from his feet by the driving force of the .45 caliber bullet.

Despite being fractionally slower, Waco proved equally—perhaps even more, under the prevailing conditions—competent!

What was more, without the need for discussion, the young blond knew to which of their enemies his companion would give attention!

While more openly vicious, neither Matthew nor Luke Warburton possessed the skill of their half-brother!

Which meant the pair were completely outclassed in such company!

Neither brother's weapon had done more than clear leather when first the right and then the left Artillery Peacemaker was out of its holster and, so close together the sounds could hardly be differentiated, roared. Caught between the eyes, Matthew died instantly. However, the younger brother fared slightly better. The lead from Waco's near side Colt caught him just below the breastbone. Letting fall his revolver, he went down seriously wounded but still alive.

"I'd say you've made your point," Doctor James Gillespie remarked, walking forward.

"It looks that way," Waco admitted. "But you'd best take a look at that old bull, just to satisfy this gent."

"Not that I reckon they deserve it, after what you told me about them," the local medical practitioner answered. "But, in keeping with the Hippocratic oath, I'd best see to those jaspers first."

"Feel free," the blond assented.

"Those two are hurt bad," Gillespie announced, having carried out the examination. "I can likely save one, or the other, if I start working on him straight away; but not *both* of them!"

"God damn it!" Doc growled, knowing the comment was directed at him. "It's getting so every time some yahoo makes me shoot him, I wind up having to dig out the bullet to save his life."

While his companion and the doctor were attending to the wounded men, Waco told Gilpin what had led up to the shooting. The cattle had been stolen from the ranch of Colonel Augustus Raines, after the Warburtons had murdered the cowhand who was driving them to the town of Backsight. Although the blond and Doc were about to return to Texas, the victim having been a friend, they had elected to hunt down the killers.

Having lost the trail of their quarry, due to a heavy

rain storm washing away the tracks, the Texans had
put to use the skills and training they had acquired
serving as peace officers under Dusty Fog.[1] Continuing
in the general direction they had been following, their
suppositions with regards to the destination of the cattle were confirmed by a cowhand they had met who
had shared a meal with the Warburtons. Not only, he
said, had the trio told him they were making for the
sale of livestock at Marana, but he had supplied a particularly accurate description of Honest David.

The latter had been the main cause of the misfor-
tune which befell the Warburtons!

Spending the previous evening looking around the
town without success, the Texans had seen the "speculator" riding toward the sale area on the following
morning. Guessing what he was up to as they had
watched him engaging Gilpin in conversation in the
bar room of the Pima County Hotel, they had decided upon a line of action. Knowing the bull "goodnighted" by Doc would be proof of their accusations,
even in the face of the fake bill of sale they had anticipated was available, they had persuaded the local
doctor to accompany them. Back-tracking Honest
David as far as the edge of the woodland, they had
left their horses in concealment and, advancing on
foot—Gillespie being a keen hunter and equally competent at silently inconspicuous movement through
the undergrowth—they had located the other broth-

---

1. See: *Footnote 7, APPENDIX ONE,* for details. J.T.E.

ers and the cattle. Wanting to make a clean sweep, they had waited until the "speculator" returned with the rancher before letting their presence be known.

"I didn't know the cattle were stolen," Gilpin stated, at the conclusion of the explanation.

"We never thought you did," Waco replied.

"It's a pity I have to lose them, though," the rancher went on regretfully. "From what I saw back there, I'll be lucky if I get any more. All the bulls I saw are being sold for more than I can afford."

"Tell you what I'll do," the blond offered. "When we get back to Marana, I'll telegraph the Colonel and tell him we've got the cattle 'n' settled things for our *amigo* those yahoos killed. Should you make him an offer, could be he'll figure it'll be cheaper to sell them to you than send somebody down from Backsight to fetch them."

"It's worth a try," Gilpin admitted eagerly. "Thanks for thinking of it."

"*Es nada,*" Waco grinned. "Handling it this way will leave Doc and me to 'tend to something else that needs doing straight off instead of waiting to hand over those fool critters."

"Howdy there, *Miss Melinder,*" greeted the taller of the two bulky men, as they crossed the dark and deserted street in the business section of the most affluent part of Tucson. "Or is it '*Miss von Rieger*'—Or, better still, '*Belle Starr*'?"

"I beg your pardon!" replied the person to whom

the question was directed, coming to a halt as the pair stopped in such a way that they blocked the sidewalk. Although good, her English had a noticeable Scandanavian timbre and she continued, "I have *never* heard of either of the ladies you speak of."

With a height of five feet eight inches, there was something in the bearing and deportment of the speaker which conveyed the impression she was even taller. Taken back in a tight and unflattering bun, her hair was blonde and added to the suggestion of Nordic birthright in her accent. The gold rimmed spectacles she wore did little to detract from her beautiful features, nor did the severe expression they bore. If the plain, almost masculine cut of her black two-piece travelling costume was intended to conceal the rich curves of a magnificent body, it failed badly. Yet she walked without in any way flaunting the full firm swell of the bosom above the slender waist and well rounded hips. She was carrying a rolled parasol in her right hand, its black covering devoid of frills or other embellishments, and the reticule gripped in her left, somewhat larger than the current fashion, was equally lacking in feminine fripperies.

Regardless of the way she was speaking and having made sufficient changes to her appearance to be acceptable in the part she was playing, Belle Starr felt sure she was in danger!

The second name mentioned by the taller man warned the blonde that her true identity was known to the menacing pair!

What was more, now Belle was able to study them at close quarters, the recognition was mutual!

Finding herself confronted by Operatives Kenneth Gill and William "Whitey" Miles, of the Pinkerton National Detective Agency, was far from a pleasant sensation for the lady outlaw!

Wearing black derby hats, dark two-piece suits, white shirts with neckties and blunt-toed boots, there was little difference in the height and bulk of the pair. Each was hard faced and neither could be termed handsome. Dark haired and swarthy, Gill was mid-European in features. Blond and heavily mustached, Miles was teutonic in appearance and, if possible, somewhat the more cruel looking. Each had on a Western style gunbelt with, respectively, a Smith & Wesson Schofield Model of 1875 and a Forehand & Wadsworth Army revolver in the holster. However, while the firearms were in fast draw rigs, Belle knew neither was a frontier trained gun fighter. They were roughhouse brawlers and, if given a chance, would prefer to defend themselves with the blackjack each carried in the right side pocket of his jacket.

At that moment, the lady outlaw was bitterly regretting having sent her intensely loyal half-Indian assistants to make the arrangements for the visit she planned to pay Tombstone!

After having taken the precaution of employing other methods for some time, since a successful "diamond switch" confidence trick had caused its victim to set a notorious bounty hunter on her track,[2] Belle was using it again while paying her first visit to Arizona Territory. Already it had proved productive and she was taking a stroll prior to bringing her latest attempt to its conclusion.

"Like hell you don't know!" Miles growled, in his guttural New York accent. "You're Belle Starr no matter what 'mother-something' name you're using to pull the 'diamond switch' down here!"

"I—I can't imagine what gives you such a foolish idea!" Belle claimed, with what appeared to be nervousness, still retaining the character of the Swedish expert on jewellery she had adopted as most suitable to gain the attention of her current intended victim. Letting the parasol slip from her fingers, she fumbled in an agitated fashion with the neck of the reticule as she continued, "But, if you don't let me pass, I shall be compelled to call for help!"

"Call all you god-damned want!" Gill authorized, his voice that of a Chicagoan, stepping closer and starting to raise his bunched right fist. "But if you even *try* to reach inside for that gun you've got in there, I'm going to bust your face so bad you'll be too damned ugly to pull your little games."

Stiffening slightly, Belle nevertheless refrained from attempting to reach the shorter of her Manhattan

---

2. Details of how the successful "diamond switch" confidence trick was carried out are given in: *CALAMITY, MARK AND BELLE.* Information regarding how another failed, in which Waco was the intended victim and Belle was indirectly involved, can be found in: *THE GENTLE GIANT.* J.T.E.

Navy revolvers which—having been modified for such a purpose—was holstered inside the reticule.[3] She did not doubt, knowing the reputation of the man making it, that the threat would be carried out if she gave the slightest excuse. However, being equally aware that the pair made a regular habit—always offering an excuse which, ostensibly, justified their actions—of mistreating prisoners regardless of age or sex, she was equally disinclined to surrender to them.

Unfortunately, without being able to produce the revolver as a means of effecting an escape, the lady outlaw could not think of any way to avoid being taken prisoner!

Even shouting for help would not serve the purpose!

Belle felt certain that, should she raise her voice, she would be silenced!

Neither operative would be willing to share the kudos for arresting such a well known member of the criminal element with the local peace officers!

Therefore, the lady outlaw would be prevented from creating a commotion which—even if leading to her arrest—could deprive Gill and Miles of the credit!

"Are these men annoying you, *mademoiselle*?"

---

3. Although, as produced by its already defunct manufacturers, the Manhattan Navy revolver had an overall length of eleven and a half inches and weighed two pounds, the one employed for concealment purposes by Belle Starr, generally in her reticule, had had its octagonal six and a half inches long barrel reduced to two inches. When circumstances allowed her to wear a gunbelt and holster, she carried another which had not been modified in such a fashion. J.T.E.

asked a precise, even prissy, male voice while Belle was still trying to resolve her predicament.

Hearing the question, Belle and the two men looked around!

Catching sight of the speaker failed to raise any hopes for her salvation for the lady outlaw!

Studying Pierre Henri Jaqfaye as he came from the alley Belle had just passed without noticing him in it, the burly operatives were no more impressed. In fact, the only emotion his presence evoked for either was annoyance that he should dare intrude upon their affairs. Regardless of the rules for conduct laid down by the Pinkerton National Detective Agency, they only showed politeness to important and influential members of the public from whom a complaint to their superiors might bring repercussions. While they recognized the newcomer as the owner of the most highly priced women's clothing shop in Phoenix, they did not consider he fell into such a category. Nor was his physical appearance sufficiently menacing to cause them to assume that tact, or conciliatory conduct was called for.

Rather the opposite, in fact!

"Just what the hell is it to *you,* fancy pants?" Gill demanded menacingly.

"It seemed your company was unwelcome to the lady, *m'sieur,*" the Frenchman replied, continuing his advance and twirling the black walking stick with a dainty, limp-wristed motion. "I felt I should ask if this was indeed the case."

"This here's law business," Miles warned, in just as threatening a fashion. "So you just get on about your 'mother-something' doings and leave us to ours!"

"You are officers of the law?" Jaqfaye asked, halting with the stick held at arms' length before him in both hands.

"What the 'something' hell do you reckon we are?" Miles challenged. "A couple of your no-bullfighter buddies?"

"Then perhaps I might see your badges?" Jaqfaye requested, sounding more like an indignant woman than a man angry over the derogatory term for a homosexual being used with regards to his friends. "And, I might add, I mean to tell your superiors I find your attitudes far from civil."

"That's not all you'll find us if you don't get the hell back to your boy friend!" Miles threatened.

"Has anybody ever told you that you have the manners of a pig, *m'sieur*?" the Frenchman inquired. "If not, it may only be because they have no wish to insult the pig!"

While Belle would have found the spirited response amusing under different circumstances, particularly as it was uttered in a high and mincing tenor, she felt it to have been highly ill-advised in the present case!

"Why you 'mother-something' lavender boy!" Miles snarled, striding forward and drawing back his left fist. "I'll—!"

Instantly, still exhibiting a suggestion of effeminate petulance, Jaqfaye met the intended attack!

Opening his left hand and swinging around the stick, although he had not removed the wooden sheath to expose the deadly blade, the Frenchman handled it as deftly—if not so lethally—as when he had killed Erroll Madden two nights earlier in Marana. Going into a lunge, he jabbed the steel ferrule at the throat of his bulky assailant. Considering what could have happened, Miles might have been grateful he was not struck by the device when it was made ready to serve its other function. However, he knew nothing of the concealed sword and was only conscious of the pain inflicted by the blunted steel tip of the stick. This proved sufficient. Letting out a startled and strangled gasp, he involuntarily changed his hostile advance into a hurried retreat.

Seeing what had happened to his companion, Gill jumped toward Jaqfaye. In one respect, at first anyway—because he was alerted to the danger—he fared better than Miles. As the stick was directed his way like a saber making a cut to the side of the head, he shot out his right hand to grasp it.

Although the distraction had offered Belle an opportunity to flee, she had dismissed the thought of doing so. She knew that her escape would leave the man who had come to her rescue at the mercy of the two burly operatives. Not that any mercy would be shown. Even as she was reaching into the reticule for her revolver, she discovered that—while he might have behaved in an ill-advised fashion so far—her rescuer was much more competent than appeared on the surface. However, watching what happened after the attack by Miles was thwarted, she concluded his luck had run out and she began to slip the Manhattan from its holster. Knowing Gill, she considered it would be needed to save the Frenchman from serious injury.

Jaqfaye proved capable of protecting himself!

Instead of being deprived of his weapon, as the lady outlaw was anticipating, the Frenchman kept hold and allowed himself to be drawn toward Gill. Suddenly swerving like a *toreador* avoiding the charge of a bull, he pivoted to swing his right foot around and toward the unguarded side of the burly operative. Such was the power behind the kick, Gill felt as if his ribs were being caved in. Releasing his hold on the stick, he blundered across the sidewalk to run face first into the wall of the building. The collision caused his derby hat to be dislodged and deprived him of its protection against what followed. Stepping into range, Jaqfaye swung around the stick. It struck the operative on top of the head and he collapsed like a punctured balloon.

Snarling half strangled profanities, Miles returned to the fray. Hoping to catch his victim unawares, he too essayed a kick. Coming around swiftly, before Belle could utter a warning or take more positive action on his behalf, Jaqfaye dealt with the latest threat to his well being. Grasping the lower end of the stick while stepping back a pace, he hooked it under the rising leg to apply a twisting heave. Sent in a twirling and headlong plunge from the sidewalk, Miles alighted on the street. Partially breaking the fall, he was just able to keep his face from striking the hard earth surface. However, this proved only a brief respite. Bounding into the air, the Frenchman came down with both feet on his shoulders. Crushed to the ground, the pain this created endured but briefly. Stepping clear, Jaqfaye turned to kick him hard on the temple and he relapsed into unconsciousness.

"Thank you, sir," the lady outlaw said, having noticed the especially vicious way in which the *coup de grace* was delivered. She had already replaced the Manhattan in the reticule and was continuing to employ the accent suggestive of Swedish "roots." "You saved me from those brutes."

"It was the only thing a gentleman could do, *mademoiselle*," Jaqfaye replied. "But now I think it would be better if we were to go away from here without delay."

"You mean before they try to attack you again?" Belle suggested, as might be expected of the kind of person she was pretending to be.

"I hardly think *that* is likely, either now or when they recover," the Frenchman declared with conviction and confidence. "I have friends of sufficient importance to ensure their employer will see to that. It is *you* I am thinking about."

"*Me?*" the lady outlaw said, looking puzzled as she retrieved her parasol.

"You, *mademoiselle*," Jaqfaye confirmed. "I doubt

that you would wish to be present if genuine officers of the law come along. After all, you *are* Belle Starr."

"God heavens, sir!" the lady outlaw gasped, although something told her that she was wasting her breath. "Surely you didn't believe all the foolishness those dreadful men were talking?"

"You play your part excellently, *Mademoiselle* Starr," the Frenchman praised. "But the man I sent to seek you out gave me an excellent description and told me where you are staying. I was on my way to visit you when I saw you might need my assistance."

"There have been times when I've needed help less," Belle conceded with a smile, reverting to her natural Southern drawl. "Shall we go, sir? I've an idea you have something interesting to tell me."

"I believe you will find it so," Jaqfaye answered, as he and the lady outlaw started walking in the direction from which she had come.

Chapter 12

THEY'RE BLAMING BELLE STARR

ALTHOUGH THE BEAUTIFUL YOUNG WOMAN WHO HAD led the gang of outlaws during the hold up of the Phoenix to Tucson stagecoach would not admit it, one of her faults was over confidence!

Having for several seconds been driving her dazed looking opponent around the boxing ring without any reprisals, the leader of the gang saw no need for caution on her part. About to deliver another blow, she was taken unawares by one which caught her in the center of the face an instant before she could launch it. Her head snapped back, pain bringing tears to her eyes and, in spite of the bulk of the eight ounce gloves tending to reduce the effect of a punch, a trickle of blood came from her nostrils.

Possessed of a completely unscrupulous nature, Sarah Siddenham was the dominant and guiding force behind the perpetration of the hold up!

Born into wealthy theatrical families with political aspirations, the band had been sent to Arizona Territory because—as a result of a complete lack of discipline while children—their frequently antisocial behavior was an embarrassment to the "liberal" pretensions of their parents. Despite having been provided with remittances sufficient to have proved adequate for their needs, provided they were willing to find some form of employment by which it could be supplemented, they had had a mutual disinclination to do so. Instead, at the instigation of Sarah, they had pooled their resources and bought a small ranch in Pima County close to the boundary with Pinal County. They had needed to take a mortgage on the property to secure occupancy, but the bank in Phoenix had been sufficiently impressed by the prominence of their families to make the required loan.

From the beginning, although this was not mentioned to the banker, there had never been any intention of working the acquired property in the conventional manner. Instead, showing considerable forethought in one respect, Sarah had claimed it might be put to more profitable use by offering it as a location where wealthy Easterners could spend vacations. Such a proposition had seemed most attractive to her companions, none of whom relished the prospect of having to perform the hard work needed to operate a cattle outfit even if they had possessed the knowledge.

It had soon become apparent there were several unexpected flaws to the scheme!

For one thing, Arizona was still far from being sufficiently settled and law abiding to attract any except the most adventurous visitors. Secondly, the Territory lacked the glamor which had attached itself—via the highly spiced stories in "blood and thunder" novels and the sensational newspapers of the day—to the Great Plains, the towns in Kansas at which the trail drives ended, or even Texas. Nor could it be reached as easily as the other three.

When an appreciation of the situation had struck home, causing recriminations and predictions of foreclosure and eviction, Sarah had showed her mettle. She had faith in the potential of the scheme, but accepted that some way must be found to keep up the mortgage repayments until this happened. Knowing no extra money would be forthcoming from their parents—all of whom repeatedly pleaded a lack of funds when the subject was raised—and being equally aware of her companions' disinclination to do any form of hard work, she had realized there was only one other way of raising funds.

Completely devoid of moral scruples and with no belief in the right of ownership except where it applied to herself and her property, Sarah had concluded crime was the only solution. Being of similar temperament, she had received only token objections from the others. While they were willing to commit robberies, all were adamant in their reluctance to facing the consequences of their crimes. They had stipulated there must be the minimum of risk to themselves and their chances of capture must be equally minimal.

With the latter in mind, Sarah had claimed their theatrical backgrounds—being unknown in the vicinity—offered an excellent means for her party to avoid suspicion. Having read of Belle Starr and her "gang," without realizing that the writer had made free use of his imagination and had made errors in naming its two most prominent male members, the strong willed young woman had asserted that a suitable disguise and the right behavior would cause the blame to fall upon the famous lady outlaw. She had strengthened her arguments by pointing out how their status locally would help the deception. As a result of their ineptitude, they were considered something of a joke in the vicinity. In fact, people in Marana and Red Rock referred to them derogatively—if not with complete justification—as the "Summer Complaints."[1] Furthermore, she had declared, there was another reason no investigation was likely to be extended in their direction.

When she had acquired the cooperation of her companions, albeit grudgingly, Sarah had sought for

---

1. "Summer Complaints": derogatory name for people, particularly those who make nuisances of themselves, taking vacations in country districts during summer. J.T.E.

the most suitable victim. To give her credit, she had displayed considerable ingenuity. Nor, considering the quality of her associates, could her strength of will and powers of commanding obedience in the face of reluctance be faulted.

Fate had stepped in to offer what had seemed an ideal proposition!

While working in disguise as a waitress at the high class Cattlemen's Hotel in Phoenix, looking into the possibility of robbing the bank to which the mortgage was owed, another prospect had attracted her. She had already contemplated holding up one of the stagecoaches which passed twice a week in each direction between Phoenix and Tucson, but her instincts warned this might prove unprofitable if selected at random. Despite all the efforts of herself and her companions, who were established in various capacities around the town, her hopes of learning when a large sum of money was to be transported in a strongbox had not materialized.

However, another prospect had arisen!

Having been informed that the man who called himself "Maurice Blenheim" wore a wig despite needing to keep his head shaved to prevent his natural hair growing,[2] Sarah had ordered increased sur-

---

2. A subsequent investigation at the instigation of Major Bertram Mosehan established that, employing a variety of aliases, "Maurice Blenheim" had carried out a number of confidence tricks throughout Arizona Territory. He always kept his head shaved and wore a wig so that, by allowing his graying hair to grow, he could alter his appearance by natural means to escape recognition. J.T.E.

veillance. On hearing he constantly went armed, including carrying a Remington Double Derringer in the crown of his hat, and wore a bulky money belt, she had concluded he could prove a profitable victim. Learning of his impending departure, she had put her plan for holding up the stagecoach into operation.

Despite the success which had attended the robbery, there had been a growing dissension among the Summer Complaints. This had not been caused by qualms over the possibility of their participation being discovered. Five days had passed without so much as a visit by the local peace officers, nor even any news regarding how the attempt to lay the blame upon Belle Starr was progressing. None of them were suffering from pangs of conscience over the murder of Blenheim. The main cause of the dissent had arisen over the division of the spoils, due to her insistence upon keeping over half of it to be used as operating expenses. Furthermore, her assumption of leadership and frequently bitter tongue had done nothing to improve relations.

Nor, as the other Summer Complaints had cause to know, did the young woman restrict herself to merely employing verbal abuse!

A vociferous feminist of the most objectionable kind, even before such an attitude reached its present stage of development, Sarah had carried her quest for equality to the extremes of seeking to acquire a knowledge of self defense equivalent to that generally considered the province of the male gender. While at a college for women in New York, along with the few others sharing her persuasions on the subject, she had taken lessons in boxing and was one of the few to attain reasonable proficiency. Keeping herself in excellent physical trim, she took great pleasure in demonstrating her competence by indulging in what she referred to as "a bout of sparring" with her masculine companions.

Although the young men had learned how painful and humiliating such contests could be, having failed to think up a satisfactory reason for refusing, "Tommy Crane" was acting as "sparring partner" shortly before noon on the sixth day.

It had soon become apparent that the bout was intended as punishment for an increasing astringence and vociferous criticism of their self appointed leader!

As Sarah was wearing only a pair of form hugging black tights, ballet slippers and bulky brown boxing gloves, the figure which had distracted the shotgun messenger for long enough to let her fell him was even more in evidence. Like Blenheim, she had worn a wig during the hold up. Her reddish brown hair was cut boyishly short. Hard, yet not unfeminine muscles played freely beneath her bronzed skin as she moved, warning of strength beyond the average. Despite perspiring freely, as a tribute to her physical condition, she was showing small sign of having indulged in four rounds of three minutes duration prior to taking the blow to the face.

The same could not be said for Dennis Orme, who had long since discarded the black wig to expose his somewhat shorter mousey brown hair and washed off the dark brown stain. Pain and the strain he was undergoing showed upon his handsome, if weak, face. Dressed in the same fashion as his opponent, what had happened to him so far had made him wish he had been less open with his resentment of her repeated comments about the inadequacy of his performance as a half Indian outlaw. Although the subject had not arisen for the past two days, he had soon discovered the "friendly workout to loosen me up" into which he had been inveigled was a serious bout as far as Sarah was concerned. Nor had being of masculine gender, if not in sexual proclivities, offered salvation. He was a far from competent boxer—improving his ability to defend himself had been her excuse for having him participate—and had taken the worst of it without, until causing the nose bleed, inflicting any significant punishment in return.

Angered by the pounding to which he had been subjected, Orme set about making the most of the opportunity he was offered to take revenge. Following the young woman as she stumbled back partially blinded by tears, he swung much more inept blows at her than she had been landing. Awkward though they might be, they arrived squarely and frequently enough to keep her off balance as she retreated and prevented her from doing anything more positive than defending herself as best she could.

Despite it being obvious that their self appointed leader was in trouble, none of the other Summer Complaints made any more attempt to intercede than they had while Orme was receiving the punishment. In fact, only the last to have put in an appearance at the scene of the crime showed anything which could be described as sympathy with her predicament.

"Stop him, Sarah!" Fiona Crenshaw yelled, but with more excitement than concern.

The impression of stocky bulk conveyed by the small "man" who had brought the horses from their place of concealment was not entirely created by the garments "he" had worn. However, the voluminous yellow "fish" slicker in particular had been selected to conceal curvaceously buxom feminine contours.

Five foot four in her Indian moccasins, pretty, her face indicative of an effervescent spirit and having shortish, curly blonde hair, the speaker moved with an agility which implied she too kept herself in good shape. Certainly the skin tight man's tartan shirt—its neck opened far enough to show she felt no need to make use of undergarments—and equally snug fitting Levi's pants she had on proved there was no flabby fat on her frame and her bare arms were well muscled. Furthermore, although she only paid lip service to the extreme feminist views of Sarah, she took an interest in self defense and regularly indulged in vigorous sessions of wrestling—generally ending in them making love—during which each strove determinedly to win, with the other girl.

Even without needing the advice from the little blonde, Sarah was preparing to do as was suggested. Requiring a brief respite in which to clear her impaired vision, her not inconsiderable knowledge of boxing advised how best to gain it. Thrusting forward between punches, she clinched with Orme and succeeded in pinning his left arm to his side. Although acting as referee, the second "half breed"— who had auburn hair and a weak, sun reddened face—did not attempt to enforce the order when she refused his call for them to break. Thomas O'Carroll knew how she was likely to respond when subjected to attempts at enforcement and had no intention of suffering the painful consequences.

Feeling the big breasts grinding against his chest, as he and Sarah bombarded one another's ribs with their free fists, Orme found the sensation more of an irritant than most men would have. Wanting to escape, the short punches he was receiving being painful, he struggled against her encircling arms.

"L—Let—g—go, you 'mother-something' bull-dyke!" the male boxer croaked, knowing he could not expect assistance in bringing this about from the referee.

Although Sarah gave signs of complying immediately, it was not out of respect for the wishes of her opponent. However, the way she responded was only partly caused by the profane reference to her by one term for the dominant partner in a lesbian relationship. She always had a compulsion to be the winner in every form of competitive activity, regardless of the methods used to attain the victory. What was more, her vicious nature demanded she repaid the punishment he had inflicted upon her.

Having acquired the time for the tears induced by pain to dry, Sarah acted. Loosening the grip of her arms, she felt Orme begin to back away. Up rose her right leg, bending so its knee passed between his thighs. A gasp of agony burst from him as, fortunately with less than her full strength, he was struck at the most vulnerable point of the masculine anatomy. Starting to fold at the waist, gloved hands trying ineffectively to reach and support the throbbing point of impact, he stumbled away from his assailant. His misfortunes were not yet ended.

Dancing after Orme, bosom bouncing with the movements, Sarah propelled her right fist up to meet his forward inclined face. In spite of the cushioning effect of the eight ounce glove, the blow crushed his nose until he felt it must be flattened across his face. Blood far in excess of that he had drawn from the girl gushed out as he was forced upright, arms dangling helplessly by his sides. Coming across with all her weight behind it, the left hand smashed against the side of his jaw. Spinning in a half circle as he went down, he crashed face first to the well padded floor. Walking over to where Sarah was hovering above him, O'Carroll started to count in the accepted fashion. Although he tried to rise, his motivation was to get away rather than continue boxing. The effort proved too much and, arms slipping apart flaccidly, he collapsed unconscious at the feet of his exultant opponent.

"Great work, Sarah!" called a masculine voice, but it did not belong to any of the male Summer Complaints.

The boxing ring was erected in a large and open fronted lean-to by the side of the ranch house. Equipped as a gymnasium, it was one of the extravagances which had caused the shortage of funds needing to be rectified—in part, at any rate—by the hold up.

Looking at the speaker, none of the Summer Complaints showed the slightest surprise or consternation on discovering he was one of the local peace officers!

Having seen what was taking place in the lean-to as he approached along the track from the stagecoach trail, Deputy Sheriff Jackson Martin had not troubled to announce his arrival. Instead, leaving his horse tethered in front of the house, he had watched the bout without his presence being suspected by any of the young people. His interest had been less in the boxing than drinking in the sight of the voluptuous female contender's naked torso made even more sensual by the black tights, curvaceous lower body and limbs.

"Th—Thank you, Jackson," Sarah replied, allowing Fiona to drape a towel across her sweat-soddened shoulders. It was an inadequate covering, leaving more exposed than concealed, but she disregarded this as she continued, "You've taken your own good time getting here, haven't you?"

"I came as soon as I could!" the young peace officer said shortly, possessing a nature which did not willingly accept criticism, staring at the still more than partially displayed breasts as they heaved up and down under the impulsion of heavy breathing to replenish depleted lungs.

"I'm sure you did," Sarah asserted, revelling in the open—if lascivious—gaze to which she was being subjected. Her words were dictated by the knowledge that she could exercise less control over the deputy than the male Summer Complaints. Ignoring her unconscious opponent, she crossed to leave the ring followed by Fiona and stood without making any adjustment to her skimpy attire in front of the newcomer. Then she asked, "Well, has everything turned out satisfactorily?"

"Not *all* the way," Martin admitted, without raising his eyes from the firm mounds of feminine pulchritude.

"I don't think I like the sound of *that*, Jackson darling," Sarah stated, and the way she spoke the name had none of the endearment in it that she used to win the cooperation of the young peace officer on other occasions. "And where didn't it go '*all* the way'?"

Without waiting for an answer, the beautiful girl started to stroll toward the nearby horse trough accompanied by Fiona. Following and finding the view from behind almost as sensual as at the front, Martin noticed that none of the other male Summer Complaints was offering to attend to the loser of the bout. Leaving him where he had fallen, they were coming to listen to what was being said.

"The sheriff of Pinal County and his posse followed your trail to where it crossed the county line and you had a break we didn't count on," the deputy explained, as Sarah shamelessly discarded the towel and started to splash the water over her perspiring torso. "I didn't have a chance to let you know, but because of that business in Coconino County, the Governor has sent an order forbidding local officers to go outside their jurisdictional areas when pursuing criminals—."

"We told you he would be chary of doing it under the circumstances," O'Carroll pointed out sullenly.

"It was better having it made official," Martin answered, showing none of the amiability with which he had addressed Sarah. "When he came to Marana, I told him I wasn't able to leave because of there being so much work with all the people in town for the cattle sale. Of course, it would have made things easier if you hadn't killed that Blenheim feller—."

"*I* didn't kill him!" O'Carroll protested.

"But, as *I* pointed out, we're all considered equally guilty of it," Sarah interrupted coldly, the attempt to disclaim guilt for the killing having been one of the bones of contention with which she had been compelled to deal since the hold up. "Anyway, it's immaterial, they're blaming Belle Starr and her gang for it."

"Not everybody's convinced it was her," Martin warned. "The driver said it was, but one of the passengers started stirring up doubts."

"Not the Senator?" Sarah asked disdainfully. "If so, I hope he was no better at it than he is at writing shorthand. None of us could read what he'd put in that pocketbook he was so eager to get back."

"Maybe I can read it," the deputy hinted, always watching for a chance to turn any event to his own use.

"Not this side of hell," the girl replied. "I threw the god-damned thing on the stove along with the money belt just in case anybody should come around to investigate us in spite of your promise they wouldn't."

"Like you promised to make sure nobody doubted it was Belle Starr and her gang," put in the man who had felled Benjamin Eckland with his Winchester Model of 1871 carbine. "It seems you weren't any too successful at doing *that*."

"Who didn't we fool, Jackson?" Sarah inquired, more to prevent unpleasantness between her male associates than out of any real curiosity.

"The youngest passenger, Franks," Martin replied, scowling malevolently at Kenneth Alan Taylor who he suspected of sharing his close relationship with the asker of the question. "We tried to close his mouth for good. But, like the stupid son-of-a-bitch he always was, Leftie botched things up so badly he broke his leg while he was running away from Franks."

"Was he—?" Sarah began, allowing the water with which she had continued dousing herself to run down and soak the tights.

"He would have been, but I killed him before he could be caught," the deputy anticipated, returning his gaze to the girl and finding, as she had surmised, the sight of the sodden garment more attractive than continuing his argument with Taylor. Having described how he had explained the killing, he concluded, "But, with all that and the other gun play there's been around Marana, I wasn't able to get away until today."

"What *other* gun play?" Sarah asked, deriving a vicarious pleasure from arousing such interest by the flaunting of her body before the peace officer in particular.

"Anyway, the sheriff of Pinal County admitted I couldn't leave town as things stood," Martin went on, after having supplied the information. "He said that it would be too late to catch up with the gang anyway, as they were heading north and would be out of Pima County before I could take a posse after them."

"Then *he's* convinced it was Belle Starr?" Fiona piped up, sounding and looking far more innocent and virginal than was the case, as she wanted to have the suppositions upon which Sarah laid plans for the hold up substantiated.

"He said he couldn't think of anybody else it could

be," the deputy replied. "I suggested that, if it wasn't her, it could be you Summer Complaints."

"You did *what*?" demanded Stanley Crowther, the member of the gang whose Winchester had helped kill Blenheim, while the other men expressed similarly alarmed sentiments.

"Would you have rather somebody else had done it and have the sheriff, or Anstead when he heard, ask *me* why I hadn't thought of you?" Martin challenged disdainfully.

"And what did the sheriff say to that?" Sarah wanted to know, showing far less concern than the male Summer Complaints, as she checked the towel she had been dabbing at her nostrils and found they were no longer dribbling blood.

"Even if he hadn't heard of you before, the rest of his posse and the local men who were there soon enough put him to rights," the deputy explained, his attitude suggesting he was drawing satisfaction and not a little amusement from the information he was imparting. "They all said none of you Summer Complaints would have the brains, even if you had the guts, to pull off such a play."

"I'm pleased to hear they feel that way about us," Sarah said, showing none of the annoyance displayed by the male members of the gang although she too was irritated by the indication of how they were regarded by people she considered to be ignorant country bumpkins. "And what did the sheriff say to that?"

"That, as you lived in our bailiwick, it wasn't up to him to look into it and I should come out here to do it," Martin replied, with less satisfaction and amusement as he thought of the derision his ploy had caused to be levelled his way. "And Anstead said the same when he arrived from the county seat and heard about it." Then, clearly wanting to change the subject before any comments could be made regarding the attitude shown toward *him* by the sheriffs of Pima and Pinal Counties, he went on, "Hey though, has that horse you turned loose at the hold up come back?"

"No," Sarah answered, guessing what had motivated the question and willing to cooperate in the interests of harmony between the men. "But it had had so many owners before us, it probably doesn't regard this place as its home."

"It was caught by those two god-damned beefheads who gunned down the rustlers, the same who claimed to know Belle Starr," Martin announced, the grimness in his tone created by remembering the treatment he had received at Waco's hands. "Nobody suggested it might be used to help trace the gang, so I was figuring on fetching it back with me. But, when I went to collect it from the office stable this morning, it was gone."

"*Gone?*" Sarah repeated, showing more puzzlement than concern.

"The greaser who looks after the horses for us probably forgot to fasten its stall last night and it's strayed, although he won't admit to it," the deputy replied, in a manner which indicated he too attached no importance to the loss. "Hell, who'd want to steal a worthless piece of crowbait like that?"

Chapter 13

WE'VE BEEN PAID TO KILL YOU

"WHOOEE!" JEDROE FRANKS BREATHED, CLOSING THE telescope as he took it from his right eye and wiping perspiration, which was not entirely caused by the warmth of the sun, from his brow. He had just witnessed the conclusion of the boxing bout in the lean-to, from a place of concealment in the woodland on a rim some half a mile away. Despite the serious intent of his observations, he had found the sight—particularly the appearance of the voluptuous female contender—interesting and not a little sexually stimulating. "Lady, even if I hadn't seen who's visiting you, I would know now that you were the 'Belle Starr' who held us up."

Deputy Sheriff Jackson Martin had been wrong in his assumption!

The horse released by Sarah Siddenham as a prelude to the robbery of the stagecoach had been stolen!

However, the theft had been carried out with the best intentions!

Being instructed to remain in Marana until an inquest upon the killing of Deputy Sheriff Alfred "Leftie Alf" Stubs could be convened, Franks had had an acceptable reason for staying!

The young Easterner had put his time to very good use!

Not only had the attempt upon his life failed, with tragic results for the intended murderer, but Franks had gained useful information from its aftermath. As there had been no mention of it having happened in such a fashion, he had not failed to notice the slip made by Martin when referring to the intruder having come to his room to try to kill him. This had warned him there must be more than just disdain for the opinions of a dude against the earlier insistence of the deputy that Belle Starr and her gang were responsible for the hold up. It had strengthened his belief that the robbers had been trying to place the blame upon the famous lady outlaw. What was more, he had concluded, everything now pointed to the local peace officers having been implicated in the scheme.

During the period of enforced inactivity, keeping a careful watch in case Martin should make another attempt to silence him, the Easterner had sought for clues which might shed light upon his self-imposed quest. He had realized that, should his suspicions regarding the involvement of the two deputies be correct, the actual perpetrators of the hold up must live somewhere in the neighborhood. He had soon received an intimation of who and where they might be. Having lost nothing in the telling, the story of Martin suggesting that the Summer Complaints could be the outlaws had struck him as significant. Regardless of the scorn being poured upon the possibility, out of consideration of by whom it was made, he had believed it was worth looking into. It was, in his opinion, exactly the tactics which the deputy would employ if he were involved with the gang. He would rely upon the very low esteem with which the young people from the East were regarded to have his suggestion scorned.

Despite having been sure that Sheriff Anstead had not been implicated in the activities of the deputies, Franks had kept his suppositions to himself when they met. Nor had he confined in Waco, Doc Leroy, or Major Bertram Mosehan, although he had frequently been in their company. His reticence in their case too had not resulted from a lack of faith in their honesty. Not only had he wanted the satisfaction of proving his theories personally, he hoped that by doing so he would achieve his ambition to become a peace officer.

Discovering how the Summer Complaints could be located had presented no difficulties. Limited though it had been, past experience had taught the Easterner that owners or hostlers of livery barns—along with barbers and bartenders—were fruitful sources of information and general gossip. It had been from the first source that he had obtained the answers. He had also been amused and flattered, as he considered it a compliment to the reputation he had established since reaching Marana, by the hostler commenting that he did not seem the kind to mix with "that bunch of useless, no account Eastern remittance yahoos and their women who're no better'n they should be." Having disclaimed any connection with them, or having any interest in them other than what he had heard about them being suspected of pulling the hold up, he hoped to avoid having his curiosity mentioned to Martin. From all appearances, he had been successful. Certainly the deputy had shown neither interest nor hostility toward him on the few occasions they had met.

At last, with the inquest over and a verdict returned in keeping with the explanation of Dubs's motives offered, Franks had been at liberty to commence the more active phase of his investigations!

Being aware that he would need to produce some form of evidence against the Summer Complaints, the Easterner had decided that the propensity of range horses to return to their home if allowed to roam free offered at least a starting point for acquiring it. The means he had adopted to bring this about could, he had realized, have proved very dangerous. Seeing him removing the animal from the small stable maintained for the benefit of the deputy sheriffs, Martin could have shot him without the risk of the real motive been suspected. However, this had not happened and, riding a horse rented from the livery barn, he had set off undetected leading his acquisition. He was clad after the manner of a working cowhand, having purchased the requisite garments from the general store, but he carried his Colt Storekeeper Model Peacemaker in its spring retention shoulder holster under his leather vest.

Following the direction he had been given, Franks had turned into the woodland from the trail as soon as he caught his first glimpse of the ranch house. Tethering the horses where they would neither be seen nor heard by anybody who chanced to ride by, he had taken the powerful telescope—one item which, having been in his small portmanteau, had not been carried off by the gang—and moved through the woodland on the rim to conduct a reconnaissance. Taking up a satisfactory position, his observations had soon convinced him that he was correct in his assumptions.

Nor had the conclusion resulted solely from the arrival of Martin.

One of the arguments against the suggestion put forward by the deputy—and which he had intended to raise himself if it was not made—had been that there were only four male Summer Complaints and the evidence of the victims indicated the woman who robbed them was supported by five men.

Studying Fiona Crenshaw as she was acting as second for Sarah between the rounds, Franks had resolved the discrepancy to his own satisfaction. Remembering the attire, particularly the yellow "fish" slicker worn by the "man" who had—apparently later than was expected—brought the horses upon which the gang had departed, he had drawn the correct conclusions. Such a garment would have been most uncomfortable in the heat and, as there was no suggestion of rain to require its waterproof protection, its only purpose was to have hidden the fact that the wearer was not of the masculine gender.

Deciding to postpone releasing the horse and sending it and its saddle—which he had also retrieved when collecting it from the stable to go down to the ranch until after Martin had returned to Marana, Franks rose with the intention of going to make sure the animals were secured for a longer wait than he had anticipated.

"They do say great minds think alike, Doc," commented a voice, in an amiable Texas drawl, although the Easterner had not heard anything to indicate there were other human beings close by.

"Why sure, Waco," answered a second speaker who was just as clearly from the Lone Star State. "Which Jed there must have figured out things just the same as *me*."

"My, this just *isn't* your lucky day, Dennis *darling*," Sarah Siddenham purred with blatantly mock com-

miseration, hauling the pile of assorted male and female garments across the table toward her. "Three of
a kind doesn't beat even an itty-bitty straight like
mine."

"I'm not much luckier," Fiona Crenshaw commented, before the even more sullen looking and now
naked loser of the boxing bout could reply. Showing
no sign of embarrassment, despite being clad in only
a pair of black stockings, she went on, "If this keeps
up, I won't have a *stitch* left to wear."

"Don't worry, dear," Sarah replied, acting equally
unconcerned although her sole attire was a pair of
lace frilled and, for the period, daringly brief scarlet
knickers. "I'm sure you and I can make a trade for
th—!"

The reply was brought to a halt by the noise of a
crash as a lock was kicked open; the front door of the
ranch house burst inward!

Holding respectively a Colt Storekeeper, a Civilian
and an Artillery Model Peacemaker—the latter one
of a brace—three masked men in cowhand clothing
came swiftly across the threshold!

The armed intrusion could hardly have come at a
more inopportune moment as far as the Summer
Complaints and Deputy Sheriff Jackson Martin were
concerned!

Although the news he had brought was not entirely
satisfactory, Sarah had considered the deputy was
still of too much importance and possible use to be
sent away discontented. Furthermore, she realized

that he knew far too much to be allowed to leave in a frame of mind conducive to betrayal. Therefore, she had asked whether he was free to stay for the night and, as an inducement, added there was to be a poker game. Having participated in such events, he had been only too willing to accept. Apart from other considerations, he had known he would have any losses he incurred returned; but would be allowed to keep his winnings.

After supper, the Summer Complaints and their guest had begun to play poker. At first, the stakes had been money. However, they had soon begun to wager the clothing they were wearing. This, as Martin had been aware when agreeing to join the game, was a prelude to a sexual orgy in which the girls gave themselves to the men with casual abandon and eagerness.

Unfortunately for the anticipation experienced by Martin as everybody began to divest garments, the latter stage had not been reached when the intrusion occurred!

"Nobody moves!" snarled the man with the Storekeeper Peacemaker, his voice harsh and suggestive of a citizen of Brooklyn in its timber. "The first to dies slow and painful!"

It said much for the composure of Jedroe Franks that he retained sufficient presence of mind, despite being startled by the sight of five men and two women around the table, none wearing more than some form of underclothing, to do as had been arranged.

Guessing from the comments, which had come as such a surprise, that no harm was intended to him, the Easterner had greeted Waco and Doc Leroy with pleasure. Then he had learned why they were present. The blond had said that, being acquainted with Belle Starr, he knew it was not her who had led the hold up of the stagecoach. Wanting to do a favor for a friend, like Franks, he and Doc were seeking to bring the real culprits to justice. It had become apparent that they had drawn similar conclusions to those of the Easterner from what they had heard in Marana. However, they had adopted different means to put their suppositions to the test.

"We *allus* do things the hard way," Doc had declared. "Which being, we concluded to follow the gang's tracks to where they was headed."

"It wasn't easy, even for a feller trained by the Ysabel Kid," Waco had supplemented. "Fact being, for 'a bunch of useless, no-account, Eastern remittance yahoos 'n' their women, who're no better'n they should be,' they'd done real good at hiding where they was headed."

"You talked to the owner of the livery barn?" Franks had guessed, remembering the description he had been given of the Summer Complaints.

"Nope," the blond had answered. "But *you* did while we was 'tending to our hosses inside—!"

"*I* don't go 'round listening to folks when they're talking private," the pallid Texan has asserted. "But there's some around who don't have *my* good manners."

"Anyways," Waco had continued, as if the interruption had not been made. "When I saw how hard it was going to be keeping after 'em, which some folks's've good manners had found it all along, we concluded to come on over to the spread and say, 'Howdy, you-all' to the Summer Complaints."

"Only we come on two hosses hid away like somebody didn't want them seen from the trail," Doc had drawled. "And, recognizing that crowbait from the hold up, *I* figured it was you who'd brought them and we might as well drop by to give you the carpetbag of yours they carried off. The money's gone, natural', but there's some other gear in it."

"Thank you," Franks had said, with genuine gratitude. "And, although I doubt if either of you have ever had this said to you before, am I *pleased* to see you."

Finding his comment had been received in the spirit it was offered, the Easterner had described what he had seen. While the Texans had agreed that everything pointed to their mutual suppositions being correct, they had also concurred with his statement when he said they still did not have any evidence to support their beliefs. After discussing ways of obtaining it, they had settled upon a plan of campaign and made preparations to carry it out.

As Martin was at the ranch house, the Texans had donned clothing from their warbags which he had not seen. Although Doc had discarded his jacket and Waco the distinctive brown and white calfskin vest, they had retained their gunbelts and revolvers. Neither was carrying spare handguns and, with the scheme they were contemplating, they were disinclined to rely upon their Winchester Model of 1876 rifles for protection.

Waiting until night had fallen, the three young men had moved in on foot. Reaching the front porch of the ranch house without being detected, Waco had employed a technique learned as a peace officer to gain admission without announcing their arrival and waiting for the door to be opened.

There were, Martin discovered, few more disconcerting sensations than to be confronted in such a fashion when wearing nothing more than a pair of "long john" underpants. Under different circumstances, he might have noticed and even drawn conclusions from the way in which the uninvited visitors were armed, if not from their attire. As it was, all he could do was join the Summer Complaints in showing amazement and alarm at the intrusion. However, also like them, he paid attention to the warning and sank back on to his chair instead of rising.

"Now that's better, you bums!" Franks asserted, refusing to allow himself to be distracted by the far from unattractive sight presented by the two all but naked girls and retaining the accent he had adopted. "Not that doing it's going to help you one way or the other. We've been paid to kill you."

"T—To *kill* us?" Thomas O'Carroll yelled, with Fiona, Martin and the other male Summer Complaints vocally registering an equal alarm at the prospect although neither he nor they made any attention to rise.

"Nobody has any reason to pay you for killing us!" Sarah claimed, no less perturbed than her companions, yet keeping her outward appearance under control.

"You try telling the jasper who owns the next ranch that he hasn't," Franks countered. "He was figuring on buying this one and it got him riled as all hell when you snuck in ahead of him to get it."

"Why didn't he make us an offer for it?" Sarah inquired, more to gain time in which to try to think of a way out of the predicament than through any real desire to learn the reason.

"He figured, happen he did, you'd heft up the price," the Easterner explained. "So he concluded it'd be a sight cheaper to pay us boys to drop in and gun you down like it was done in a robbery."

"We—We've got money here—!" Dennis Orme croaked.

"S—Sure we have!" Stanley Crowther supported in a quavering falsetto squeak, waving a hand at the table top. "T—Take it all and let us l—live!"

"Why that wouldn't be right 'n' honest by the gent who's hired us," Franks answered. " 'Specially for the chicken-shit you've got there."

"Th—Th—There's a lot more you can have!" Kenneth Alan Taylor offered and the other male Summer Complaints nodded agreement.

"Tell your boss that we'll sell!" Sarah snapped, glaring at the men with a mixture of anger and disgust for their cowardice.

"Oh sure!" Franks scoffed. "And lose all that good pay he's going to give us for killing you off?" He paused and glanced around the table, then continued, "Rufe, start with that son-of-a-bitch with the swelled up nose!"

"Yo!" Waco responded, the single syllable word offering no clue as to his place of origin.

"N—No!" Orme squealed, rising as the masked blond walked toward him cocking the staghorn handled Artillery Peacemaker. "N—No! For god's sake, Sarah! Give them the money from the hold—!"

"How much do you want to leave us alive?" the taller girl asked, before her former opponent could complete his suggestion.

"We come high," Franks warned.

"How high?" Sarah said sourly.

"Five thousand dollars ought to do it," the Easterner decided. "With what's on the table, that is."

"We don't—!" Sarah began.

"Kill him!" Franks ordered.

"No!" Orme screamed and lunged across the table with his hands reaching for the taller girl. "Give it to them, you 'mother-something' bull-dyke!"

Shoving back her chair, Sarah rose before the panic stricken man could touch her. Throwing a look of disgust at him as he sprawled face down on the pile of clothing she had been gathering after winning the pot, she gave a sigh of resignation and said in a bitter voice, "I'll fetch it for them, but don't start whining at me for doing it."

"Go and watch her, Jesse!" Franks instructed. "And keep this in mind, Big Apples,[1] should you try anything sneaky, we'll cut down every last son-of-a-bitch here and both of you gals, after we've done funning with you."

"Do just what they tell you!" Crowley commanded, although—knowing the taller of the girls—the words sounded closer to pleading.

With the other poker players reiterating the advice, Sarah walked dejectedly away from the table. Followed by Doc, who halted in the doorway, she went into the bedroom she shared with Fiona except when giving her favors to one of the men. Taking the key from inside her pillow, she pulled a small strongbox from beneath the bed and unfastened it. Raising the lid, her eyes went to the Merwin & Hulbert Army Pocket revolver on top of the money. However, knowing it would not serve her purpose, she made no attempt to reach for it.

"Five thousand, wasn't it?" the girl asked, turning her head.

"Back off and stand facing the corner," Doc answered, putting a snarling timber to his voice and raising it to a higher than normal pitch.

For a moment, Sarah thought of grabbing for the

---

1. Used in this connotation, the word "apples" meant breasts. J.T.E.

revolver. Then, once again, common sense overcame the desire. She knew that, although she might—in fact, probably would—kill the man in the doorway, the other two were sure to get her. Certainly she could not rely upon any of her companions, with the possible exception of Fiona, risking a similar fate to come to her assistance. Yielding to the inevitable, she did as she had been told. Halting in the corner, she stood looking over her shoulder. She was seething with impotent rage as she watched Doc removing and tucking the money into the front of his shirt. It was obvious he was not counting it to obtain the sum agreed upon, nor had she expected him to. When he had removed all the contents, he backed out of the room with the Merwin & Hulbert dangling in his left hand. Following him, she found all her companions had been sent to stand facing the wall farthest from the table and the other two masked men were pocketing the not inconsiderable amount of money which had remained on it.

"Was there enough for us?" Franks inquired.

"And more," Doc confirmed, deliberately keeping his response brief in spite of using the assumed tone.

"Let's go then," the Easterner instructed. "I don't reckon, dressed so fancy, any of you good folks will be figuring on rushing straight out after us. But, happen you get the notion to start shooting our way as we're pulling out, I wouldn't was I you. If you do, we'll come back and burn this place down 'round your ears."

"Well," Waco said, as he and his companions reached their waiting horses without there having been any hostile reaction from the house. "We've got a fair piece of the loot back. Which same, afore anybody tells me, we can't prove's how it is the loot. So we'll just have to count on them going after some more, the same way they got it."

Chapter 14

WHAT IS YOUR INTEREST IN HIM?

~~~

"M'SIEUR LE COWBOY FROM TEXAS, WILL YOU PLEASE carry my baggage to ze best hotel for me, *veuillez*?"

Hearing the words in a feminine voice which could only be directed at him, Waco turned from where he was pretending to read a notice on the board by the front door of Arizona State Stage Line's depot in Phoenix. Although they had been uttered with a strong suggestion of a French accent, there was something about the voice which struck him as familiar. Wondering why this should be, he ran his gaze over the speaker as she descended with the aid of the shot-gun messenger out of the stagecoach from Tucson which had just arrived.

Such were the alterations Belle Starr had made to

her appearance since they last met, it took the young blond a couple of seconds' close scrutiny to identify her!

Not only had the lady outlaw changed the blonde wig for one of black hair held in a chignon, discarded the gold-rimmed spectacles—worn to establish her character in Tucson and also vary her appearance from the last occasion when she had met Waco[1]—and stained her skin an olive brown pigmentation, but she was clad in a much more eye-catching and color-ful fashion. No longer was she attempting, or rather giving the pretense of attempting, to hide her mag-nificent figure. The travelling costume she had on was revealing to the point of being risqué. What was more, much expensive looking jewellery glinted and glistened ostentatiously on her ears, neck, wrists and hands.

"Why it'd surely be a pleasure, ma'am," the blond asserted truthfully, controlling his surprise as well as the lady outlaw had expected would be the case and also justifying her confidence in his intelligence by giving no sign that they were acquainted. "Just point her out when she's took off and I'll tote her where-all ever you want."

"You will be most careful with them, *m'sieur*, won't you?" Belle asked, pointing to the two expen-sive looking brown leather portmanteau which the

---

1. We have no record, at this time, of when or where the "last occasion" a meeting between Belle Starr and Waco took place. However, details of their first encounter are given in: *THE GENTLE GIANT*. J.T.E.

driver was removing from the rear boot of the vehicle and placing upon the sidewalk with much greater care than was usually the case with his unloading. "The rest of my jewellery is in them, as is the five thousand dollars I have brought for travelling money."

"You're toting *five thousand dollars* around, ma'am?" Waco inquired, noticing the words had been uttered far louder than might be considered advisable if such a sum was in the portmanteau.

"But doesn't *everybody*?" the lady outlaw countered.

"*I* for sure *don't*, ma'am!" the young Texan declared, also speaking louder than was necessary. Glancing along the sidewalk while picking up and discovering that the bulky portmanteau were heavy enough to be well filled, he went on in no quieter a tone, "Fact being, I've never even seen a whole five thousand dollars in one pile."

"I could hardly believe my eyes when I saw you as the stage was coming in," Belle stated, in a much lower tone and resuming her normal Southern drawl, as she and Waco were walking away from the depot. "And I'm really pleased to see you."

"Now it's real pleasurable to hear you say so," the blond drawled. " 'Cause this's the *second* time it's been said to me in less'n a week."

"I suppose there has to be a *first* time for *everything*," the lady outlaw smiled. "Are Mark, Dusty and Lon with you?"

"Just Doc," Waco admitted. "And I'd bet all I've got in my pocket against your five thousand dollars in these bags I can guess why you'd be wanting *Dusty and Lon* to be around."

"Go ahead," Belle challenged, without needing to ask why the first name she had used was not included.

"You're here looking to say, 'Howdy, you-all' to the gal who's been trying to make folks think you and 'your gang' robbed the stage between Red Rock and Marana," Waco assessed. "Which I reckon Blue Duck and Sammy Crane must be counting themselves real important, being part of your 'gang.' Don't you have them around?"

"Not hereabouts," Belle admitted. "You know, much as I hate to admit it, I always knew you were smart. But I didn't know you ran to second sight."

"How's that?"

"Weren't you waiting for me to arrive?"

"I can't come right out truthful' and say 'yes' to that. I was watching that yahoo dressed up so he reckons everybody'll mistake him for a cowhand as's dogging along our trail."

"He walks more like one of those strange little men who think they're girls," the lady outlaw commented, having halted so as to convey the impression she was looking into the window of the shop they were passing. In reality, she had studied Dennis Orme for a few seconds and also the street beyond him. "But I doubt if that's why you find him so interesting."

"You doubt *right*," Waco replied. "I only like gals when they are gals."

"Then what is your interest in him?" Belle wanted to know.

"Could be the same's you'll have in him," the blond asserted with confidence, as Belle and he started walking once more. "Have I won my bet?"

"You have," the lady outlaw confirmed and all the levity had left her voice. "I don't take kindly to having some god-damned lobby-Lizzie trying to have *me* blamed for crimes *she's* doing."

Which was true enough!

However, there was another reason for Belle to be hunting the gang who had robbed the stagecoach!

Having accompanied Pierre Henri Jaqfaye to his shop, the lady outlaw had had her supposition confirmed that he was far more than appeared on the surface. Although his sexual proclivities were more masculine than his behavior suggested, he had made no attempt to prove the fact. Instead, he had been all business and proved he was very competent in his— at least on the surface—subsidiary business. Admitting frankly he was an important member of an organization planning to control all criminal activity first in Arizona Territory and then, if successful, throughout the United States, he had explained how their ambitions had been placed in jeopardy by the indiscrete behavior of Senator Paul Michael Twelfinch II. Pointing out how she could be endangered by the woman pretending to be her while robbing the stagecoach, particularly as a passenger was murdered, he had asked what she intended to do

about the situation. On being informed that she
meant to go in search of her rival, he had asked if she
would find out what happened to and, if possible, retrieve the incriminating pocketbook. She was not in
favor of the aims of his organization, suspecting these
could threaten the independence of people like herself,
but the renumeration she had been offered added to a
desire to clear her name had led her to agree.

Having had her specialized requirements satisfied—the clothing and expensive looking jewellery
being produced by the Frenchman from his stock—
and being promised a free hand, Belle had made her
plans. Knowing their presence might inadvertantly
give her away, she had telegraphed Blue Duck and
Sammy Crane in a simple code, telling them to go
into hiding until she contacted them. Then she had
booked a seat on the next stagecoach from Tucson to
Phoenix. Although she had been supplied with the little information available to Jaqfaye, lacking the
added details which had become known to the Texans and Jedroe Franks, her instincts and knowledge
of criminals had led her to assume the State Capital
would offer the best starting point for her quest.

As she had said, on her arrival from Tucson, the
lady outlaw had seen a potential ally in whatever lay
ahead. Nor had she doubted that Waco would offer
his services, which was why she had asked him to
carry her baggage. In fact, she had already heard
enough to believe he was in the State Capital engaged
upon a similar mission to her own. The prospect was

most satisfying to her. Until the meeting, she had been undecided as to what action she would take if she succeeded in locating the gang. With him by her side, she would not need to wait until she could send for her two men to join her.

Yet, despite knowing that—being a very close *amigo* of the only man who had ever and would ever have her love[2]—the young Texan was completely trustworthy and would never divulge anything he heard, Belle had a code of conduct by which she lived and it precluded her from telling him of the organization. For all that, in the not too distant future, he would play a major part in its downfall without needing any assistance or information from her.[3]

"Well now, could just be you've made a start at finding her already," Waco drawled. "Trouble being, you looking so fancy and talking about the money you've just lost to me, you've got more than one feller on your trail."

"You mean that loudly dressed, red faced dude across the street," asked the lady outlaw, having noticed more than Orme while conducting her examination.

"Why sure," the blond confirmed, grinning in admiration. " 'Cepting, 'though he looks and talks like he's from lil ole New York seeing's how he hails from thereabouts, and isn't dressed so quiet and tasteful as some of us good ole Texas boys, he's *segundo* of a pretty fair-sized spread—as such are judged in *Arizona*."

---

2. See *Footnote 1, APPENDIX TWO,* for details. J.T.E.
3. Told in: *Chapter Three, "The Petition," WACO RIDES IN.* J.T.E.

"And he's a friend of yours?"

"He's got that honor—Happen 'honor's' the word you'd use."

"I *wouldn't*," Belle said dryly, finding herself unable to resist falling into the kind of banter which frequently passed between the members of Ole Devil Hardin's floating outfit no matter how grave the situation. "But don't stop telling it so *modestly*!"

"He's Pete Glendon," Waco obliged. "Only we're no so close *amigos* as I made it sound, seeing's I haven't found a chance for us to make *habla*. Was I asked, though, I'd reckon he's after pretty much what we are."

"Do you mind if I ask why you think that way?"

"No, ma'am."

"All right then!" the lady outlaw was compelled to say when no information was forthcoming. "Why?— And just you wait until the next time I see Betty Hardin. You know how us girls stand together."

"You wouldn't do nothing so ornery 'n' mean's to set her on my trail?" Waco asked, in well simulated horror, being aware of how effectively Elizabeth "Betty" Hardin could deal with those who she felt had not behaved in a satisfactory fashion.[4] "Not that I'm scared, mind—!"

" 'Dear Betty,' my letter will start—!" Belle claimed, sounding ominous.

---

4. Information regarding Elizabeth "Betty" and her relationship with General Jackson Baines "Ole Devil" Hardin can be found in various volumes of the *Civil War* and *Floating Outfit series*. She also "stars" in *Part Three, "It's Our Turn To Improvise, Miss Blaze," J.T.'S LADIES.* J.T.E.

"Calf rope, ma'am!" the blond responded, making the traditional cowhand expression of surrender. "Like I said, not that I'm scared mind, but here-all's how I read the sign."

"You've done well," the lady outlaw praised, after the Texan had told of what had happened since Doc Leroy and he had belatedly become involved in the holdup of the stagecoach. "But is that man following us, the trying-to-be cowhand, I mean, the 'woman' who led the gang?"

"Nope, just one of the lil Injuns," Waco corrected. "The big chief's a *woman* sure as you are and, unless I'm missing my guess, a pretty smart one."

"I'm looking forward to meeting her," Belle stated. "Where is she at?"

"Right here in town," the blond replied. "Fact being, 'most all the gang are around and about. Which I'm real relieved they are."

"Why?"

"Way we took all that money from them, I got to figuring after we'd done it the fool way *Doc* picked out, there was a chance we'd throwed such a scare into them's they'd head back East so fast you'd reckon their butts was burning. Which isn't what you'd be wanting."

"I want my fingers in her hair!" Belle said savagely.

"Was I all mean and ornery, like *some* as's close by," Waco drawled. "I'd keep quiet and let you go ahead unknowing. But, being all noble, forgiving and good—!"

"Betty Hardin!" the lady outlaw reminded.

"Natured," the blond continued, as if the interruption had not happened. "I'll just say you'd best watch her real good while you're doing said grabbing hold. Doc and me got there just too late to see it, but Jed told us she's a better'n fair hand at fisticuffs."

"Fisticuffs?"

"They get into what's called a 'boxing ri—'!"

"I know what 'fisticuffs' are, but do you mean *she* does?"

"She whomped that yahoo following us real good, way Jed told it," Waco explained. "And, when we bluffed them into handing over the money, it was her that all those knobheads turned to for it."

"I'll keep it in mind, should we lock horns," Belle promised, knowing she had received a genuine warning. "Where is she?"

"Working at the Cattleman's Hotel, along of the lil blonde gal's runs with her pack," Waco supplied. "One of the men's there, as well, playing like a guest."

"Do you think we could persuade some of them that confession is good for the soul?" the lady outlaw inquired, having considerable respect for the judgment of the young cowhand as she knew him to be far shrewder than his levity suggested was the case.

"Likely, seeing's how Lon's taught me some of his Grandpappy Long Walker's Comanch' tricks and you've likely learned a few from those part-Indian boys of your'n," Waco guessed. "Least-wise, we could get at least some of the *hombres* and most likely the lil blonde gal talking—to us. Trouble being, some god-damned law-twisting son-of-a-b—gun might tell whichever it was to say they was lying 'cause they was scared when they got into court and it'd only be our word against their'n. Which I don't reckon *you'd* be wanting to get into the witness stand, comes to that."

"I *wouldn't*!" Belle admitted vehemently. "The Pink-Eyes[5] are too close on my heels for that and, after what happened to two of them back in Tucson, I wouldn't want to let them lay hands on me."

"Then we'll have to make a stab at getting them to show their hand," the blond asserted. "And, was I asked, going by the way you're dressed and jewelled, not to mention bawling at the top of your voice about that five thousand dollars you've just now lost to me, I'd say that's what you was figuring on doing all along."

"It was," the lady outlaw confirmed.

"Which only goes to prove's how great minds think alike," the blond declared. "Because Doc, Jed and me've been working along that same trail."

"I see it's the Cattlemen's Hotel you're taking me to," Belle remarked, before any more of the scheme could be described.

"It's the best place in town," Waco replied. "Only you won't be getting your fingers into her hair there,

---

5. "Pink-Eye": a derogatory name for an operative of the Pinkerton National Detective Agency. J.T.E.

not unless you go into the bar room. Which for-real ladies aren't allowed in, even if they sound like they're French."

"I'll keep *that* in mind, too," Belle promised. "How will I know them?"

"Anyways, happen you aren't sure," the blond finished, having described Sarah Siddenham, Fiona Crenshaw and Thomas O'Carroll as they now appeared. "I'll have Doc point them out for you."

"What's he doing?" the lady outlaw asked.

"Being a professional gambling man," Waco replied. "He's doing right well at it and they're watching him."

On arriving at their destination, Belle reverted to her French manner of speaking. Presenting the blond with a dollar, for "being zo kindly," she gave her attention to the desk clerk. Pocketing the coin and grinning, Waco strolled outside and found his path was blocked.

"Howdy, Pete," the blond greeted, noticing William "Fast Billy" Cromaty hovering to one side in an ideal position to assist the foreman in case of gun play. "I hardly knowed you, all dressed up so quiet and fancy."

"I've allus been knowed for my good taste," Glendon answered, being clad in a pearl gray derby hat, a black and white check suit with a mauve vest, a salmon-pink shirt to which was attached a celluloid collar, a necktie of numerous clashing colors and black town boots with white spats. However, he was still wearing his gunbelt. "That was a right nice lady you toted the bags for. Do you know her from somewhere?"

"She never even told me her name," Waco replied, with complete truth. "Gave me a whole dollar, though."

"That was mighty generous of her," the foreman said dryly. "How's about you, me 'n' Fast Billy going off some place where we can make us some talk?"

"Now that's right strange," the young Texan drawled. "I was just fixing to say the self-same thing to you."

Chapter 15

THIS IS A HOLD UP, I'M BELLE STARR

"OH MY GOOD GOD, CHARLEY!" FIONA CRENSHAW
suddenly screeched, clutching at her mid-section.
"Stop the coach, my time's come and I'm starting!"

Listening to and watching the buxom little blonde,
Belle Starr, Waco, Doc Leroy, Jedroe Franks and
Peter Glendon were each willing to concede she was
an excellent actress!

Accompanying the foreman and William "Fast
Billy" Cromaty to a sparsely occupied saloon in the
less affluent section of Phoenix, the blond young
Texan had found sufficient privacy to satisfy his and
their mutual curiosity.

Without divulging too many details, as Major
Bertram Mosehan had stressed the need for discre-

tion concerning the force of peace officers being formed until they were ready to commence operations, Glendon had done the majority of talking for himself and the lanky cowhand. Claiming the injured shotgun messenger was a friend, which was true although they had not seen each other since their Army days, he had said he was hoping to flush out the gang who had robbed the stagecoach between Red Rock and Marana. He was posing as a whiskey drummer, hence his gaudy attire, who would be carrying a large sum of money upon his person when he left town.

Admitting to having an identical motive where the lady outlaw was concerned, but refraining to mention how recently they had been in each other's company, Waco had told the two men as much as he had passed on to her. He had found they had reached similar conclusions with regards to the Summer Complaints and Deputy Sheriff Jackson Martin, even before having seen Sarah Siddenham, Fiona and the male members of the group in Phoenix. They had laughed heartily on learning of the source from which had come the money being used by Doc and Franks for a similar purpose to that of Glendon. In addition to what he had won since his arrival, being an excellent poker player with an equally thorough knowledge of fair and cheating methods in many forms of gambling, the slender Texan was displaying a sizeable bankroll where various of the Summer Complaints could see it. For his part, particularly in the same company, the Easterner had boasted of how

he tricked the outlaws into believing he was poor
when he had had over five thousand dollars belonging to his employer hidden in the cheap trunk they
had not thought to search.

On Glendon having suggested—with the full
agreement of Cromaty—that they all worked together from then on, Waco had not hesitated to give
agreement on behalf of himself and his two companions. He was satisfied the pair would do, as
cowhands on a trail drive often said when referring
to one of the most hazardous conditions they could
encounter while moving a herd of half wild longhorn
cattle, "to ride the river with when the water was up
over the willows."

Still without betraying her true identity, despite his
belief that Glendon and Cromaty would not turn her
over to the authorities, nor trust him the less for
being her willing accomplice, the blond had said the
"rich lil ole French gal" planned to return to Tucson
on the Friday stagecoach. When he had suggested
they made their attempt to capture the gang on the
same vehicle, Cromaty objected on the grounds it
would put the "foreign lady" in jeopardy and the
foreman had given his concurrence. The young Texan
had countered this by pointing out that Dennis Orme
had already seen her jewellery and heard the refer-
ences to the "five thousand dollars travelling
money," so the gang might decide to rob the stagecoach upon which she was travelling without the
added inducements they intended to offer as bait. De-

claring they would do everything possible to avoid harm befalling the "French gal," Waco had won his way.

Following the lines of action already set in motion, the conspirators had soon felt sure they were achieving the desired results. With the exception of the blond, who was keeping in the background and not setting himself up directly as a prospective victim for robbery, the men had each noticed various of the Summer Complaints paying careful attention to their activities. Meeting Waco by arrangement, Belle had said the same applied to her. Having contrived to be selected for the comfortable role of hotel guest, Thomas O'Carroll had tried to make her acquaintance and advised against displaying so much jewellery or talking about the "travelling money."

On Wednesday, satisfied all was ready, the conspirators had respectively announced in the hearing of the Summer Complaints that they intended to go to Tucson by the Friday stagecoach!

Of the young Easterners, only Fiona and Stanley Crowther had been in sight on Thursday morning!

Arriving at the depot of the Arizona State Stage Line early Friday morning, Belle, Doc, Franks and Glendon had discovered that the little blonde and Crowther were also travelling as passengers. Without being able to discuss the matter, each of the intended victims had guessed how the stagecoach was to be stopped for the hold up to take place.

Clad in a cheap black "spoon" bonnet shaped like

the rear end of a Conestoga wagon's canopy, a threadbare brown coat over a gingham frock and high buttoned shoes, Fiona looked like the wife of a poor farmer. The hat covered all her hair and she had removed the heavy make-up employed while working as a saloongirl in the bar room of the Cattlemen's Hotel. What was more, by careful padding and a walk appropriate to such a condition, she had given the impression of being in a well advanced stage of pregnancy. Wearing a cheap suit, collarless white shirt, heavy black walking boots and round topped, circular brimmed black hat such as was worn by members of the Grange,[1] Crowther was also a sufficiently good actor to pass as the kind of husband she would be expected to have.

Studying the pair when he joined the stagecoach, Waco concluded only one thing prevented them from being completely convincing in their disguise. The hands of each were far too clean and soft for the type of people they were supposed to be.

Wanting to lessen the chance of their complicity being suspected, the blond had ridden to Red Rock on horseback accompanied by Cromaty and another of the cowhands enrolled as a member of the proposed force of peace officers. Brought to the vehicle on its arrival, apparently in a drunken stupor, he was loaded aboard by his companions. Then, looking so

---

1. "Grange:" the order of Patrons of Husbandry, a nationwide association of farmers in the United States founded in 1867 for the furtherance of agricultural interests. J.T.E.

vacant such blatant indiscretion appeared believable, the lanky cowhand had requested Toby Winkler—the shotgun messenger replacing Benjamin Eckland until he was recovered from his injuries—to "make sure good ole Davey-boy gets off safe at Marana, 'cause he's toting five hundred dollars belonging to his boss."

Once on board, Waco had continued to behave as if sleeping off excessive drinking by sprawling along the center seat which had been lowered. He was helped in his pose by being held in position with the knees of Doc, Franks and Glendon at the rear and Belle, who had agreed to let the "married couple" have the window places, in front. As had been the case throughout the journey so far, there was only desultory conversation such as might occur between travellers with little or no common interests. However, while passing through the woodland about a mile beyond the boundary between Pinal and Pima Counties, having either recognized something or seen a signal which had escaped the attention of the other passengers, the little blonde had let out her realistic sounding comment.

"*What?*" Crowther gasped, displaying an equally well simulated alarm. Then, leaning out of the window he had asked to be allowed to sit next to on boarding the vehicle, he raised his voice. "Driver! Driver! For god's sake, stop!"

"Why?" demanded Walter Tract from the box, impressed by the suggestion of dire urgency in the speaker's voice.

"I—It's m—my w—wife!" the male Summer Complaint answered, contriving to appear close to panic stricken. "S—She's s—starting to have the baby. Please, for god's sake, stop right *now*!"

"Well I'll be damned!" the driver ejaculated, not entirely without a trace of satisfaction in his voice, as he started to haul back on the ribbons and apply the brake. "I've finally got it happening to *me*!"

"Which being, I surely hope *you*, that fancy French gal, or one of them fellers inside knows how to haul the little sucker out should it conclude not to come natural-like!" Winkler replied. " 'Cause I've never so much's seen one being born and ain't 'special keen to do it now."

Such was the feeling of awe experienced by bachelors in particular where the female process of giving birth was concerned, neither Tract nor the guard gave a single thought to the kind of precautions they would have taken—particularly in an area offering so many places of concealment on either side of the trail—if there had been a request for the stagecoach to be halted for almost any other reason. As it was, regardless of the sentiment he had uttered, Winkler lay the Greener shotgun behind him on the roof of the vehicle and swung down from the box with alacrity. Showing an equivalent dearth of wariness, the driver descended just as quickly from the other side.

"This is a hold up. I'm Belle Starr!"

The words were shouted in a feminine Southern drawl from the right side of the vehicle, as the two employees of the Stage Line were turning toward the doors.

Reaching for the Colt holstered on his right thigh, Winkler was intending to dart around the rear of the stagecoach when he saw a movement from the corner of his eye. Looking more closer, he discovered that two masked and armed men were moving forward from where they had been hidden behind nearby trees. Their attire, weapons and the shoulder long black hair of the taller warned him that they were part of the gang which had carried out the earlier hold up. Even without being covered by the revolver and Winchester Model of 1873 carbine they were respectively carrying, mindful of his responsibility to avoid putting the passengers in jeopardy, he would not have attempted to complete his draw. Instead, he raised his hands to shoulder level in a sign of surrender.

Looking over his shoulder, Tract also refrained from trying to arm himself. He found he was staring into the muzzle of the Winchester carbine, this time held by the second "half breed," which had killed Maurice Blenheim. At the other side of the bulky trunk of a white oak tree where they had concealed themselves, was the "blonde" who made the announcement. However, she now wore a masculine black shirt, Levi's pants, moccasins and was bareheaded. Although she had not displayed any weapons on the previous occasion, she now held the Merwin & Hulbert Army Pocket revolver which—the driver was unaware—had been dropped on the porch of the ranch house by Doc Leroy on the evening the loot from the previous hold up was taken from the Summer Complaints. There was, Tract noticed, no sign of the "white outlaw" who had supported the "half breed."

"Sit where you are, all of you!" Crowther commanded. Having withdrawn his head after making the request for the stagecoach to be halted, he had reached behind his back beneath the jacket. Bringing out the Colt Storekeeper Model Peacemaker he had carried there unsuspected—or so he believed—as he was speaking, he went on, "Stay put, you men, or 'Frenchie' there gets gut-shot!"

"By my 'husband,' or by *me*!" Fiona supplemented, thrusting her right hand into what appeared to be a pocket but was actually a slit allowing access to the interior of the carefully padded gingham dress and extracting another of the short barrelled Peacemakers. Pointing it at Belle and drawing back the hammer with both thumbs, she continued, "So you'd all best do as you're told!"

"Whatever you say, ma'am!" Doc drawled soothingly, seeing the suggestion of alarm which came to the face of the lady outlaw as the weapon was fully cocked in such an inexpert fashion. "That's some *baby* you've had!"

"Isn't it?" the little blonde giggled, being of an ebullient nature and regarding the hold up as little more than an enjoyable game.

"Send them out one at a time, Josie, Vince!" Sarah Siddenham called brusquely. "And don't be all day about it—you-all!"

"Sure, 'Belle!' " Crowther assented, remembering the instructions to establish the "identity" of the "blonde" leader of the gang beyond all doubt. "You heard the lady, drummer. Get up and haul your ass out of here!"

"Ladies first, damn it!" Fiona protested. "Get up and let us through, St—Vince!"

"Sure!" Crowther grunted and rose, pressing himself back against the wall of the stagecoach's body.

"All right, 'Frenchie,' " the little blonde commanded, too excited to notice how calmly the other female passenger was accepting the situation. "Push by that drunken sot and get out!"

"Whatever you say, madame," the lady outlaw replied in her thick French accent and started to obey.

The two Summer Complaints failed to appreciate it in their inexperience, but they were putting themselves in particular in jeopardy by their behavior. Neither Fiona nor Crowther was able to maintain an adequate covering of the three men occupying the rear seat as "Frenchie's" departure was being made. However, although Doc and Glendon—even Franks to a lesser degree—were offered opportunities which the first two were fast enough to have made the most of, all remained passive.

"Where the hell's all that fancy jewellery you-all allowed she wears?" Sarah asked, as Belle preceded Fiona from the vehicle.

"She said she'd taken the advice she was given and hid it with her 'travelling money' in her bags," the little blonde replied, the lady outlaw being clad in the plain black two piece costume and white blouse she had worn on the night she met Pierre Henri Jaqfaye, unadorned by the excellent quality costume jewellery which he had supplied. "I'll wrestle you for the pick of it."

"*You-all* watch what you're doing!" Sarah snapped, knowing how irresponsible the excitable little blonde could be even in situations of grave danger when a serious attitude was necessary. "Move toward the back of the coach, 'Frenchie!' "

"Whatever you say, '*Miss Starr*!' " Belle answered, her accent wavering a little due to annoyance.

"Come on out, you fellers!" Sarah instructed, as the men from the other side of the vehicle appeared escorting the shotgun messenger. "Come easy and with your hands empty. My other two boys are covering *you-all* and 'Frenchie' with their rifles from where *you-all* can't see them, so don't try anything!"

" 'Scuse me, Miss Starr, ma'am!" Tract put in, before the order could be obeyed.

"Well?" Sarah asked.

"Iffen I shed my gun, can I go stand by the heads of the lead team?" the driver requested. "Last time, they come close to bolting when some shooting started."

"Do it!" Sarah authorized. "Only, if you-all fancy try-ing anything smart while you're taking that hawg-leg out, just mind what I said would happen to 'Frenchie!' "

Watching the driver remove his revolver with obvi-ous disinclination to use it as an offensive weapon, the self-appointed yet no less efficient leader of the Sum-mer Complaints felt a half conceived thought nagging at her. However, she was prevented from trying to bring it to completion. Instead, she swung her atten-tion from the disarmed Tract as he did as he suggested to the open right side door of the stagecoach.

Rising and keeping his hands held so there was no suggestion that he might be contemplating hostile ac-tion, Doc walked by Crowther. Using part of the money taken from the Summer Complaints, he had had the black cutaway coat he was wearing tailored so it of-fered a similar access to his ivory handled Colt Civilian Model Peacemaker as would his ordinary jacket. In spite of that, he had no intention of taking action until the time was more suitable. Jumping to the ground, he went to where Belle and Tinkler were standing.

Showing a caution equal to that of the pallid fea-tured Texan, although each was offered a similar op-portunity to render Crowther *hors de combat* at least temporarily due to his negligence while being passed, first Franks and then Glendon quit the vehicle. Drop-ping to the ground, each in turn went toward the rear of the stagecoach.

"Miss Belle *Boyd*!" the lady outlaw called, as the foreman was emerging, having scanned the surrounding terrain with eyes trained to locate hidden enemies and having drawn conclusions from the scrutiny. "Please ask your *three* hidden outlaws to be very careful with their *revolvers*. I would not wish to be shot, even by accident."

"Don't let it worry you any, 'Frenchie,' " Sarah replied, so engrossed in keeping watch upon her companions rather than the victims of the hold up—as she never trusted them to perform any task adequately—she failed to notice the discrepancies in the request. "They'll not bother you none, so long as those jaspers with you behave."

"Then I hope they will behave *properly*," Belle declared, being willing to bet she had achieved her purpose.

From what she could see, the lady outlaw was convinced the rest of the Summer Complaints had shown an equal lack of perception. Like Sarah, none of them commented upon her having being wrong with regards to the number and weapons of the "hidden outlaws." Nor, it seemed, had they noticed how she had used the name of Belle "the Rebel Spy" Boyd instead of her own.[2]

---

2. Details pertaining to the career and special qualifications of Belle "the Rebel Spy" Boyd can be found in: *THE COLT AND THE SABRE, THE REBEL SPY, THE BLOODY BORDER, BACK TO THE BLOODY BORDER, THE HOODED RIDERS, THE BAD BUNCH, SET A-FOOT, TO ARMS! TO ARMS! IN DIXIE!, THE SOUTH WILL RISE AGAIN, THE QUEST FOR BOWIE'S BLADE; Part Eight, "Affair Of Honour," J.T.'S HUNDREDTH, THE REMITTANCE KID*—in which she "stars," although this volume is listed in the *Calamity Janes* series for convenience—*THE WHIP AND THE WAR LANCE* and Part Five, *"The Butcher's Fiery End," J.T.'S LADIES.* J.T.E.

Everything, Belle told herself, now depended upon whether the male "victims"—Waco in particular—drew the correct conclusions from what she had said!

And upon the Summer Complaints not having called upon Deputy Sheriff Jackson Martin to play a more active part in their latest robbery!

If this was the case, the peace officer had concealed himself so well he defied being located!

By doing so, Martin would supply the Summer Complaints with a most potent ace in the hole!

The deputy could, in fact, turn the tables completely against the lady outlaw and her companions!

Chapter 16

TWO BELLE STARRS ARE *ONE* TOO MANY

INSIDE THE STAGECOACH, JUST AS OBLIVIOUS AS Sarah Siddenham and the rest of his associates that he had heard an opinion being given, Stanley Crowther stood eyeing Waco disdainfully!

Since his arrival in Arizona Territory, the Summer Complaint had frequently suffered humiliation when brought into contact with cowhands due to their disinclination to accept unproved his belief that he was a person of greater intelligence and capabilities than themselves. Such incidents, bruising his over-inflated ego, had left him with a considerable bitterness and antipathy where they were concerned. His one attempt to assert himself had ended so painfully and quickly, he had never had sufficient courage to try again. However, finding himself with one of the disrespectful breed apparently at his mercy, he realized he was being granted an opportunity to take at least partial revenge.

"Come on, you drunken son-of-a-bitch!" Crowther growled at the recumbent and unmoving blond haired Texan, nudging him with a knee. "Wake up, god-damn you!"

When the words and jolt produced no effect, the Summer Complaint gave a grin of delight. Satisfied he was safe from reprisals while doing so, he tucked the Colt Storekeeper Model Peacemaker into his waist band, this time at the front. Grasping the breast of the open necked shirt with his right hand, he intended to raise the head and shoulders of his seemingly defenseless victim and bring a return to consciousness by slapping the tanned face.

Before Crowther could advance his scheme beyond gripping the front of the shirt, he received a shock similar to that which had so disconcerted Benjamin Eckland during the preliminary stages of the previous hold up!

Cold as the blue of a Texas sky just before the eruption of a summer storm, the eyes of the intended victim opened!

There was no suggestion of recovering dazedly from a drunken stupor in the gaze!

As had been the case with Eckland, an appreciation of what was portended by the sight caused Crowther to jerk away!

The Summer Complaint was no more successful than the shotgun messenger had been!

Rising swiftly on either side of his right arm as he was releasing the shirt involuntarily, Crowther felt two powerful hands grasp the lapels of his jacket. As they started to jerk forward, Waco twisted his lower body and slammed the right knee into the small of Crowther's back.

Such was the speed, force and completely unanticipated nature of the attack, there was nothing the Summer Complaint could do to counter it!

"It's a trick!" the Texan bellowed, as his efforts were propelling the startled Easterner away from him. "Kill him!"

Hearing the commotion, Sarah, Fiona Crenshaw and their male associates outside the stagecoach looked in its direction. At the sight of a shape coming through the open door at some speed, not one of them waited to make an identification. Believing Crowther had given the warning, every Summer Complaint acted upon it. Turning from the people they were covering, two Winchester Model of 1873 carbines and three assorted handguns bellowed almost simultaneously. Not all were pointed with anything approaching accuracy. In fact, only a blunt nosed .44 bullet[1] from

---

1. As the cartridges of the Winchester Model of 1873 was center- and not rim fire, which were used in its predecessors, the Model of 1866 and the Henry, it was considered a precautionary measure to mold the bullets with a truncated head. If jolted, one with a conventional point might strike the firing cap of the next ahead in the tubular magazine and cause a premature detonation. J.T.E.

the shoulder arm which had killed Maurice Blenheim and one of more conventional shape, with a caliber of .45, discharged by Sarah found their intended—if incorrectly selected—mark. They were, nevertheless, sufficient. Caught in the chest and head while still falling from the vehicle, either injury being fatal, their recipient was dead before he arrived on the ground.

A belated realization of what they had done caused the surviving Summer Complaints, with the exception of Fiona, to start returning their respective weapons to the previous alignment!

Granted the diversion they desired, the intended victims of the hold up set about making the most of it!

First into action was Doc Leroy!

Coming out and crashing with such speed only one man was *almost* capable of equalling,[2] the pallid featured Texan's ivory handled Colt sent a bullet into the head of Dennis Orme as he was working the lever of the Winchester which had just killed for the second time.

Slightly slower, but ahead of the others, Peter Glendon brought the Remington New Model of 1874 Army revolver from its cross draw holster. Although he did not intend such leniency, its bullet crippled the right arm of Thomas O'Carroll before the second carbine could be fired again.

Lacking the competence of the men around him

---

2. Although all evidence indicates Captain Dustine Edward Marsden "Dusty" Fog, *q.v.* was unbeatable at drawing two guns simultaneously, Marvin Eldridge "Doc" Leroy was fractionally faster with one. J.T.E.

where fast gun handling was concerned, Jedroe Franks was nevertheless third into action. However, on twisting the Colt Storekeeper from its spring retention shoulder holster and throwing a shot at Kenneth Alan Taylor, he made an error in tactics which had proved fatal for more than one man in similar circumstances. Although the bullet grazed the Summer Complaint's left side, eliciting a yell of pain and causing him to stagger a couple of paces, he still kept hold of his Colt. What was more, he showed indications of being willing to use it. Despite seeing this, having had time to think what he was doing instead of merely reacting by instinct to circumstances, the young Easterner could not bring himself to respond due to the realization that such an act would cause the death of another human being.

Fortunately for Franks, neither Doc nor Glendon harbored such scruples. Each was aware of the danger. Knowing Taylor was behaving in the fashion of a cornered rat, both met the threat in the fashion of trained gun fighters. Turning, their respective revolvers thundered at almost the same instant. Killed instantly, the bullet sent by the Summer Complaint in his last moment alive was deflected just above the head of the young Easterner.

While Toby Winkler was almost as competent as the slim Texan and the stocky foreman, his sense of duty prevented him from joining them in the drawing of revolvers!

Instead, the shotgun messenger devoted his efforts

to protecting what he imagined to be a female passenger who was defenseless and probably too scared to do anything in that line by herself!

Silently praying that her belief that no members of the gang were hiding close by was correct, Belle Starr had reached into the reticule at the first sign of trouble. Even as her right hand was starting to slip the Manhattan Navy revolver from its holster, she felt herself grasped and swung around to be pushed away from the rear end of the stagecoach. Spluttering a furious exclamation, despite realizing why she was being treated in such a fashion, she fetched out the weapon while regaining control of her movements. Coming to a halt, she swung her gaze to find out what was happening.

Giving only scant attention to the male Summer Complaints, all of whom were being dealt with by her companions, the lady outlaw devoted her interest to the two young women. Only one struck her as being likely to give trouble; but it was the one against whom she had the greater animosity.

Knowing the men she had brought into the desperate situation, Sarah had no faith in either their courage or their ability as gun fighters. Even before the lack of the latter was made obvious, she concluded there was nothing to be gained by making a fight; particularly in contention against men who were clearly most skilled in matters *pistolero*. As usual with her, to think was to act. Instead of trying to use the Merwin & Hulbert Army Pocket revolver, she turned and fled toward where their horses had been left.

Seeing the woman who had tried to have her blamed for robbery and murder was running away, Belle tossed down the reticule. With her left hand reaching toward the waist band of the black shirt, she set off in pursuit. However, she was not allowed to catch her quarry without interruption.

Amazed by the way in which things were suddenly and terrifyingly going wrong, Fiona had allowed the revolver she had fired—to miss Crowther and remove Walter Tract's hat in passing—to fall from her hand. Seeing the "French woman" apparently rushing at her, but being unaware that she was not the objective, she was sufficiently spirited to try to meet what she believed to be an attack. Having no interest in the little blonde, whose motives and status in the gang she had deduced accurately, Belle lashed a backhand slap with the left arm which sent her spinning aside and ran on.

Not very far, however!

Giving a squeal of pain mingled with rage, Fiona hurtled after her assailant!

The first intimation received by the lady outlaw of the second attempt at intervention came when she felt her skirt being grasped from behind. Having been prevented from doing so by the blonde's first try, she had once more put her left hand to preparing to make use of a modification to the garment which she had copied from Belle "the Rebel Spy" Boyd. A tug at the fastening of the waistband caused it to loosen and open sufficiently wide for the skirt to be discarded more quickly than by conventional means. Having it grabbed by Fiona, who had dived and was falling, made the function perform even more rapidly.

Although Belle felt her movements being impeded, the skirt was sufficiently voluminous so that when it opened it failed to trap her completely. Staggering, but without falling, she contrived to liberate first the right and then the left leg. In doing so, exhibiting the tight fitting black riding breeches and Hessian leg boots beneath the discarded garment, she was compelled to make a half turn. What she saw warned she was not yet finished with the attentions of her assailant.

Having landed upon hands and knees, displaying a rubbery agility regardless of her buxom build, Fiona bounded to her feet and into the attack once more. Despite admiring her spunk, the lady outlaw was disinclined to accept any further delay in going after the leader of the gang. Stepping to meet the intended assault, she made effective use of her longer reach. While she swung another back hand blow, this time it was with the right fist. This held her revolver, but it was the knuckles and not the barrel or frame which made the contact. Struck at the side of the jaw, the little blonde made another involuntary twirl away from her objective. On this occasion, however, she was unable to remain on her feet. Stunned by the blow, she pitched face forward on to the ground and lost all interest in the proceedings for several seconds.

Resuming her twice interrupted pursuit, Belle ran through the trees in the direction she had last seen the taller girl disappearing. Although she scanned her surroundings, she could not locate her quarry due to the dense undergrowth. However, the crack of revolver shots from ahead gave her an indication of where to go. Other sounds, following the three detonations, warned why the weapon had been discharged.

"God damn it!" the lady outlaw ejaculated, coming into a clearing and seeing Sarah riding away; also that the shots had frightened off the horses belonging to the other Summer Complaints. "You'll not get away from me that easy, you bitch!"

"They do say it's the first sign of going *loco*," Waco drawled, having left his companions to deal with the situation at the stagecoach and followed Belle, "when folks start talking to themselves."

"I'd love to hear what Betty Hardin says to *you* after I've written her!" the lady outlaw answered. "Help me catch one of their horses, please. *Two* Belle Starrs are *one* too many and I'm aiming to make sure it stops!"

Although she had not heard anybody approaching the ranch house on horseback, Sarah Siddenham was more curious than alarmed when she heard its front door open!

Not for the first time, the over confidence which was the chief weakness of the Summer Complaints' otherwise competent leader was causing her to under-estimate the gravity of her situation!

Satisfied she had prevented all chance of an immediate pursuit by scattering the rest of the horses, none of which was the equal of her own mount in quality, Sarah had not seen anything to make her revise the opinion as she was fleeing from the disastrous attempt to hold up a second stagecoach. Instead of taking the kind of circuitous route and employ the methods of hiding tracks learned from Deputy Sheriff Jackson Martin—although these had not been successful, as they failed to prevent Waco from following the Summer Complaints to their headquarters—she had returned by the quickest route. Leaving her badly lathered horse to take care of itself on her arrival, she had entered the ranch house to carry out the plans she had made during the flight from Pinal County. Feeling certain that any of the gang who survived would not hesitate before betraying her, with the probable exception of Fiona Crenshaw, she knew she must not delay her departure. In fact, but for one vitally important consideration, she would not have returned at all.

The theft of the money on the night of what the Summer Complaints referred to as a game of "strip-poker" had proved to be a blessing in disguise. While it had led to Sarah and her companions electing to carry out the second hold up, despite having learned the neighboring rancher had no designs upon their property, it had improved her own situation in one respect. She had lost her "table stakes," but this had affected her far less than any of the others. Not only had she frequently emerged a winner from earlier conventional poker games, but she had abstracted some of the loot put aside for the furtherance of their scheme. As the money had been hidden separately in her bedroom, it was not included in the sum stolen by the three masked intruders. Added together, winnings and abstractions would be more than sufficient to let her escape from the immediate vicinity long before the stagecoach could be taken to either Red Rock or Marana and the authorities informed, then to continue her flight out of Arizona.

Tossing the bag containing the money on to the bed alongside the blonde wig she had removed, Sarah started reaching for the Merwin & Hulbert revolver more as a precaution than with any belief she might need it.

"Leave it where it is, 'Belle Starr!' "

Hearing the feminine Southern drawl from the door of the room, Sarah tensed as she looked over her shoulder. For a moment, as the newcomer had discarded the black travelling costume, the wig and was barefoot, explaining how the silent approach had been possible, she failed to recognize the "French woman" from the stagecoach. What she did notice immediately, however, was the short barrelled weapon resembling a Colt 1851 Navy revolver which was lined unerringly at her. There was something in the demeanor of the new arrival, whose blonde hair was cropped as short as her own—a requirement created by the need to wear wigs in the hot climate of

Arizona—warning it would be extremely unwise to disobey.

"Who are you?" Sarah demanded, raising her right hand clear of the Merwin & Hulbert and turning slowly until facing the door.

"You've lost your Southern drawl, *you-all*," replied the genuine Belle Starr. "It wasn't very well done, at that."

"I said who are you?" Sarah hissed, although she was beginning to suspect the truth.

"I'm Belle Starr," the lady outlaw answered. "And, as I told a very good friend just recently, I don't take kindly to lobby-lizzies trying to have me blamed for their crimes."

"What do you intend to do with me?" Sarah challenged, despite feeling *very* uneasy as she listened to the softly spoken words. "Take me into Marana and turn me over to the sheriff?" She paused, then continued. "But, *if* you did that, I would just as quickly turn *you* over."

"You'll be in no condition to turn *anybody* over," Belle claimed. "Fact being, *Summer Complaint,* by the time I'm through with '*you-all*,' you're not going to be doing *anything* for longer than it will take *me* to be long gone to where the sheriff, or anybody else, can't find me."

"You talk *big* for somebody with a gun in her hand," Sarah countered, employing all her considerable strength of will to prevent her trepidation showing. She was helped by the timber of disdain with which the words, *"Summer Complaint"* were said. Glaring defiantly at the visitor, she continued, "Which is about *all* I could expect from a 'mother-something' peckerwood tail peddler like *you!*"

"Come on out here and close the bedroom door behind you," Belle instructed, gesturing with the Manhattan and showing no sign of the annoyance she felt over being referred to by the derogatory names for a Southron and a prostitute. Moving backward as she was speaking, although not sufficiently to prevent her from keeping the weapon lined on the other girl, she concluded, "Then we're going to see just how much I *need* a gun to hand you your needings!"

"Now what?" Sarah demanded, having done as she was instructed.

"I'm going to give you the licking of your life," the lady outlaw declared, crossing to open the center drawer of the sidepiece. Placing the Manhattan in and closing it, she went on, "But you can make things a whole heap easier for yourself if you hand over the pocketbook you took from Senator Twelfinch."

"Can I though?" Sarah said disdainfully. "Now isn't that a *pity,* peckerwood. I burned it as soon as we got back here. So I'll just have to pass up having things made 'a whole heap easier' for me."

"I'm pleased to hear it," Belle claimed, the attitude of disinterest assuring her that the other was speaking the truth and also unaware of the potential value offered by the incriminating contents of the book. "I'd hate not to be able to give you *everything* you have coming."

With that, the lady outlaw started to cross the room!

Watching Belle approaching, a surge of elation flowed through Sarah. Until she had seen the revolver put away in the drawer, she had had fears for her life or at least her future liberty. Now she believed both were secure. Clearly the "peckerwood" believed there was nothing to fear at her hands. In which case, she was confident she could cause a most painful disillusionment.

Bringing up her fists as she had learned when boxing, but without eliciting a similar posture of readiness, Sarah danced rapidly to meet her opponent. Out shot her right fist, for a jab to the "olive brown" face of the beautiful Southron. Such a punch, she felt sure, would come as a complete surprise and be sufficiently disconcerting and hurtful to render its recipient open for more punishment.

Disillusionment came quickly!

Not, however, as had been envisaged by the Summer Complaint!

Warned by Waco of Sarah's competence at boxing, Belle was not taken unawares and was ready to defend herself. Rising, her hands caught the approaching wrist before the knuckles could make contact. Raising the trapped arm, she pivoted beneath and jerked it downward. A wail of alarm burst from

Sarah as she felt herself suddenly being spun in a half somersault through the air. Coming down on the dining room table, it collapsed under her weight and sent her rolling across the floor. Before she could recover her wits, two hands sank into back hair and, with a wrench which threatened to rip hanks out by their roots, jerked her erect. Swung around by it, she had hurtled across the room on being released. This time, however, she was more fortunate and her spinning rush ended with her sitting on the well padded sofa by the side of the room.

Following the Summer Complaint, Belle concluded she was far from finished. Bouncing from the sofa, she was ready to take action before the lady outlaw arrived. Knotting her fists, Belle shot out a right, a left and another right in rapid succession. Showing she had recovered from the surprise received on her opening attack, Sarah deftly blocked each blow in turn. On the heels of the third thwarted attempt, the Summer Complaint retaliated by hooking two punches into the unguarded midriff of the lady outlaw. Gasping, the blows having been hard, Belle was driven back a couple of steps. Before she could pass beyond reaching distance, a backhand slap to the side of the head sent her spinning to land on hands and knees facing away from her assailant.

Hissing in triumph, Sarah advanced spraddle-legged to sit on Belle's back as if riding a horse. Having gained the position, she used each hand in turn to box the other's ears. Such tactics were all very well when used in a friendly rough and tumble with Fiona, as they had proved on two occasions, but they were less effective against an opponent whose intentions were far from friendly. Letting out a squeal of pain at each slap, Belle thrust upward against the straddling legs. Such was her strength, she raised the Summer Complaint from the floor and, by tilting over, sent Sarah back to it in a far from triumphant sprawl.

Although the pair separated, this only lasted for a moment!

Coming to their knees, the lady outlaw and the Summer Complaint faced each other from less than two feet apart. Acting as if upon a signal, they thrust inward and, with a thwack of colliding flesh, they flung their arms around one another in a violent embrace. Tumbling sideways, locked in that fashion, they went across the floor in a rolling mill which made them appear to be one misshapen human form trying to destroy itself. Skill was forgotten and pure instinct as primeval as the beginning of time prevailed. Fingers clawed at flesh, but neither had nails of sufficient length to inflict scratches. However, cloth tore and buttons flew from masculine shirt and female blouse as they were grasped and wrenched at mindlessly. Involuntary grunts and moans burst through clenched teeth as arms and legs squeezed with savage power, sounding louder in the otherwise silent room.

Having attained the upper position, straddling

Sarah with fingers sunk like talons into the bosom now bared by the loss of the shirt, Belle gained the first serious advantage; but only momentarily and she paid for it. Pure chance rather than deliberate intent caused Sarah to drive her wildly flailing right fist against the temple of the lady outlaw. Toppling sideways, hand clutching at the point of impact, Belle rolled desperately away from the Summer Complaint. The blow had been devastating, a "shot to the head" of the kind which frequently won boxing bouts. Nor was the lady outlaw unaware of the danger.

Could Belle recover, she wondered as she was struggling to rise, or would Sarah attack again before her strength returned?

The answer came quickly!

Coming up fast, the Summer Complaint pounced like a chicken hawk stooping to take an incautious hen. Still with none of the skill she possessed, she grabbed and flung Belle to the floor. Going forward, she caught hold of the lady outlaw's right leg as it and its mate kicked in a futile attempt to fend her off. Raising the limb, she gave a squeal more animal than human and sank her teeth into the calf. Even through the riding breeches, Belle felt the pain. It galvanized her into a reprisal which her condition might otherwise have failed to produce. Kicking with all her strength, she was not too bewildered to ensure the contact was made with the top and not the toes of the left foot. The force of the impact sent the Summer

Complaint spinning against the wall, from which she flopped to the floor.

Once again, the embattled pair rose almost simultaneously. Legs trembling under the exertions, they paused for a moment to re-marshal their strength for the next confrontation. Then they rushed at one another with a fury which was astonishing and not a little frightening to behold, if there had been any spectators. For close to ten minutes without a pause, they twisted, grabbed, yanked, punched and generally mauled each other without mercy. Soaked in perspiration, each shedding blood from nostrils, lips and grazes, they went at it as if their lives depended upon it. In one respect, at least where Belle was concerned, it did. Should she fail, she believed Sarah would kill her out of hand.

Coming to their feet, still without releasing their clutches, the girls reeled heedlessly across the room. Locked in the same fashion, they crashed through the window taking glass and sash with them. By some miracle, neither was cut by the shattered shards. However, tumbling to the porch served to jolt them apart. Not for long, however. Lurching erect, they closed. Slightly faster, Belle delivered a kick which sent the ball of her foot into the pit of Sarah's stomach. Gasping for breath and badly hurt, the Summer Complaint began to double over. Her throat descended into the clutching hands of the lady outlaw and she was forced upright once more.

Now Sarah was in jeopardy!

Held by the savage constriction of the strong fingers wrapped around her throat, the Summer Complaint squirmed in desperation to free herself and to breathe. Flailing with her fists and trying to kick, she beat at her assailant's head and body with a decreasing force. For her part, the lady outlaw took the blows and devoted every ounce of her will power to keeping up a pressure which grew harder to maintain by the second. Feeling her fingers trembling from exhaustion, as the clutching efforts strained at her muscles, she suddenly thrust Sarah away. Colliding with the wall of the house, what small relief the Summer Complaint experienced was short lived.

Swinging around to give it more force, Belle's clenched right fist buried its knuckles into the mound of Sarah's left breast until seeming to force it into her chest. As the fist withdrew, the left hand crossed to force the right breast outward. Torment too great to be fought off flooded through Sarah. Her eyes rolled until only the whites showed and her mouth opened in a soundless scream of agony. Such was her pitiful condition, she did not feel the right cross to the jaw which flung her half naked body as flaccidly as if its bone structure was removed to measure its length on the hard planks of the porch.

Stumbling with the force she had exerted, right hand feeling as if it was broken so hard had she delivered the final blow, magnificent—if now raw looking and bruised from the punishment it had taken—bosom heaving as she struggled to replenish her lungs, Belle caught the rail of the porch for support. Through the whirling mists of pain and exhaustion which assailed her, although she had not heard anybody riding up, she heard a drawling masculine voice.

"I told you she was good!"

Raising her head, despite her right eye being swollen almost shut and the vision through the left impaired by tears of pain and exhaustion, the lady outlaw could not envisage any sight more pleasant at that moment than Waco and Doc Leroy hurrying toward her from where they had left their horses—brought after the stagecoach by William "Fast Billy" Cromaty and the other cowhand—standing ground-hitched and hurried toward her. Opening her mouth to make some response, she felt her legs buckling and she crumpled unconscious alongside the girl she had beaten.

Chapter 17

YOU'VE GOT YOURSELF TWO *TEXANS*

❦

"The sheriff's got that deputy of his locked in the pokey along with those two gals and the one yahoo who come through alive," Peter Glendon said, at the completion of the report he was making. "It was him, not the gals who told us about Martin. Fact being, the big 'n's got a busted jaw and isn't talking and the lil blonde's so worried about her being beat up the way she is, she won't say nothing."

It was noon of the day following the attempted stagecoach hold up which had seen the brief criminal career of the Summer Complaints brought to an end.

On regaining consciousness, after having had her injuries attended to by Doc Leroy—who had also diagnosed and treated Sarah Siddenham for the jaw broken by the final blow of the fight—Belle Starr had made arrangements for her future. She had spent the night at the ranch house and, at sun up that morning, took the best of the available horses and, wearing some of her opponent's clothing, set off to by-pass Marana and report to Pierre Henri Jaqfaye in Tucson. However, she had not mentioned this to the Texans; claiming only she had to collect the property left on the stagecoach. As she was confident she would arrive before the vehicle, she would allow the Frenchman to repossess it. They had brought her skirt and reticule and, as none of her own property was in the portmanteaus, she was not unduly worried in case he was unable to do so.

Delivering Sarah to Marana, Waco and Doc had found Sheriff Anstead was in charge. He accepted the reason they gave for the "French woman" not having accompanied them, being pleased to have the whole of the Summer Complaints either in jail or awaiting burial at the undertaker's establishment. He had, he claimed, been on the point of going to the ranch to take their leader into custody and was saved the ride.

On leaving the sheriff's office, the Texans had been met by Glendon with an offer to join him for lunch. Arriving in the dining room of the Pima County Hotel, they had found they were not the only guests. Looking very pleased with himself, having just received a chance to achieve his ambition to become a peace officer—although he did not mention this—

Jedroe Franks was sharing a table, set apart from the other occupants, with Major Bertram Mosehan.

"What did you say the name of that lady Pinkerton agent was?" Mosehan inquired, looking from Doc to Waco and back.

" 'Magnolia Beauregard,' " the young blond supplied, knowing this was a favorite alias of the lady outlaw.

"But she didn't show you anything to prove she was what she claimed?" the major asked, face as lacking in emotion as if it was carved from stone.

"Well, no sir, she didn't," Doc replied. "Fact being, she wasn't in any shape to do more than lay quiet and let me 'tend her hurts when we got there."

"She told us her name was 'Magnolia Beauregard' and she was a Pink-Eye though," Waco supplemented, having asked Belle to do this so he would not be speaking untruthfully—as far as it went—by giving the information. "And, her being a lady and all, it wouldn't have been right to make out we didn't believe her."

"I suppose not," Mosehan said dryly. "Well anyway, Belle Starr's name has been cleared."

"I reckon she'll be right pleased when she hears about it," Waco drawled, with such innocence it seemed butter would be hard put to melt in his mouth.

"Could the OD Connected spare you boys for a while longer?" Mosehan inquired, deciding enough had been said upon the subject regardless of his very accurate suppositions about the true identity of "Magnolia Beauregard."

"I reckon they could, hard as *that* is to believe," Waco affirmed. "About *me,* anyways."

"What he means," Doc commented, in tones of patient martyrdom. "I reckon Ole Devil and Dusty would reckon they could do without *me* and be a whole heap better off if somebody close by I could name wasn't around, happen there was a good cause for us staying away."

"I'm beginning to wonder if it's worth it!" the major informed Glendon somberly. Becoming more serious, he quickly explained the task he had been appointed to carry out and then went on, "So I'm organizing a small force of State Police who'll be able to go everywhere in Arizona and I could use a couple of fellers like you."

"*Us!*" Doc breathed. "In the *State Police?*"

"I mind what Davis's carpet-bagging State Police did in Texas during Reconstruction,"[1] the young blond growled. "And, much as I'd like to take cards in your game, major, there's no way I'd wear a badge with *State Police* on it!"

"Or me!" the slender cowhand supported.

"All right," Mosehan replied, considering that gaining the services of the two extremely competent young men would be worth making the adjustment.

---

1. An example of how a life was ruined by the persecution of the State Police in Texas during the Reconstruction period following the War Between The States is given in: *THE HOODED RIDERS.* J.T.E.

"We'll have 'Arizona Rangers' on our badges and warrants of authority."[2]

"That being so," Doc declared. "You've got yourself two men!"

"Better than that," Waco stated. "You've got yourself two *Texans*!"

---

2. By a remarkable coincidence, the first captain in a later and better known force of Arizona Rangers was called Burton C. "Cap" Mossman. J.T.E.

IN CONCLUSION

THE READER MAY BE WONDERING WHY THE PRESENT
"expansion" differs so drastically from the episode
which first appeared in THE HARD RIDERS.

When we asked Dustine Alvin "Cap" Fog about
this, he said the descendants of Major Bertram Mosehan at the period in which our source of information
was produced felt it unwise to allow the true facts to
be known; particularly in connection with the escape
of Belle Starr. However, "Cap" and Andrew Mark
"Big Andy" Counter persuaded the present generation that their illustrious forebear's memory would
not be affected adversely by the disclosure of what
really happened and permission was granted for us to
do so.

APPENDIX 1

Left an orphan almost from birth when Waco Indians—
from whence came the only name he ever knew—raided
the wagon train in which his parents were travelling,
Waco had been raised as a member of a North Texas
rancher's large family.[1] Guns had always been a part of
his life, starting with an old Colt Model of 1851 Navy
revolver and progressing through a brace of Colt 1860
Army[2] to two Colt "Peacemakers."[3] Leaving his
adopted home shortly before his sixteenth birthday, he
had become a member of Clay Allison's "wild onion"
CA ranch crew. Like their employer, the CA cowhands
were notorious for their reckless and occasionally dangerous behavior. Living in the company of such men, all
older than himself, he had become quick to take offense
and well able, eager even, to prove he could draw his
guns with lightning speed and shoot very accurately. It
had seemed only a matter of time before one shootout
too many would see him branded as a killer and fleeing
from the law with a price on his head.

Fortunately for Waco, that day did not come!

From the moment Captain Dustine Edward Marsden "Dusty" Fog saved the youngster's life, at considerable risk to his own, a change for the better had

come.[4] Leaving Allison, with the blessing of the Washita curly wolf who wanted to see him attain a better life, Waco had become a member of the OD Connected's floating outfit.[5] The other members of this elite group had treated him like a favorite younger brother and had taught him their respective specialized skills. Mark Counter gave him instruction in bare handed combat. The Ysabel Kid had shown him how to read tracks and perform other tricks of the scout's trade. From a friend who was a gambler, Frank Derringer,[6] had come information about the ways of honest and crooked members of his profession.

From Dusty Fog, however, had come the most important lesson of all!

When—Waco already knew *how*—to shoot!

Dusty had also supplied advice which, helped by an inborn flair for deductive reasoning, turned Waco into a peace officer of exceptional merit. Benefiting from such an education, he became noted in law enforcement circles. In addition to the periods during which he wore a badge under the Rio Hondo gun wizard,[7] he served with distinction in the Arizona Rangers,[8] as sheriff of Two Forks County, Utah[9] and finally as a United States Marshal.[10]

---

1. How Waco repaid the obligation to his adopted father, Samuel "Sunshine Sam" Catlan, is told in: *WACO'S DEBT*.

2. Although the military sometimes claimed—probably tongue in cheek—it was easier to kill a sailor than a soldier, the weight factor of the respective weapons had caused the United States Navy to adopt a revolver of .36 caliber while the Army purchased and employed the bulkier .44. The weapon would be carried on the belt of a seaman and not—handguns hav-

ing originally and primarily been designed for use by cavalry—on the person or saddle of a man who would be doing the majority of his travelling and fighting from the back of a horse. Therefore, .44 became known as the "Army" caliber and .36 as the "Navy."

3a. Introduced in 1873 as the Colt Model P "Single Action Army" revolver, but more popularly known as the "Peacemaker," production continued until 1941 when it was taken out of the line to make way for the more modern weapons required in World War II. By that time, over *three hundred and fifty thousand* were manufactured in practically every handgun caliber—with the exception of the .41 and .44 Magnums, which had not been introduced during the first production period—from .22 Short Rimfire to .476 Eley. However, the majority were chambered to fire the .45 or .44-40. The latter variety, given the name, "Frontier Model," handled the same ammunition as the Winchester Model of 1873 rifle and carbine.

3b. The barrel lengths of the Model P could be from three inches in the "Storekeeper" Model, which did not have an extractor rod, to sixteen inches for the so-called "Buntline Special." The latter was also offered with an attachable metal "skeleton" butt stock so it could serve as an extemporized carbine. The main lengths of the barrels were: Cavalry, seven and a half inches; Artillery, five and a half inches; Civilian Model, four and three-quarters inches.

3c. Popular demand, said to have been caused by the upsurge of action-escapism-adventure Western series on television, brought the Peacemaker back into production in 1955 and it is still in the line.

4. Told in: *TRIGGER FAST*.

5. "Floating outfit": a group of four to six cowhands employed by a large ranch to work the more distant sections of the property. Taking food in a chuck wagon, or "greasy sack" on the back of a pack mule, they would be away from the ranch house and unsupervised by their employer for long periods, so were the pick of the crew. Because of the prominence of General Jackson Baines "Ole Devil" Hardin in the affairs of Texas, the floating outfit of the OD Connected ranch were frequently sent as a whole or in part to assist such of his friends who found themselves in difficulties or endangered.

6. Frank Derringer makes a "guest" appearance in: *COLD DECK, HOT LEAD* of the *Calamity Jane series*.

7. How Waco gained his training and experience serving as deputy marshal under Captain Dustine Edward Marsden "Dusty" Fog, *q.v.*, is told in: *THE MAKING OF A LAWMAN, THE TROUBLE BUSTERS, THE GENTLE GIANT, THE SMALL TEXAN* and *THE TOWN TAMERS*.

8. Waco's career with the Arizona Rangers is covered in: *SAGEBUSH SLEUTH, ARIZONA RANGER, Part Six, Waco series, "Keep Good Temper Alive," J.T.'S HUNDREDTH* and *WACO RIDES IN*.

9. Told in: *THE DRIFTER* and, by inference, *DOC LEROY, M.D.*

10. Told in: *HOUND DOG MAN*.

APPENDIX 2

Over the years we have been writing, we have frequently received letters asking for various Western terms, or incidents to which we refer, to be explained. While we do not have the slightest objection to receiving such mail, we have found it saves us much time-consuming repetition to include those most often requested in each volume. While our "old hands" have seen them before, there are always "new chums" coming along who have not.

———

1. We are frequently asked why it is the "Belle Starr" we describe is so different from photographs which appear in various books. The researches of Philip José Farmer, q.v., with whom we consulted, have established that the person we describe is not the same as another, equally famous, bearer of the name. However, the Counter family have instructed Mr. Farmer and ourselves to keep her true identity a secret and this we intend to do. How her romance with Mark Counter commenced, progressed and was brought to an end is told in: *Part One, "The Bounty On Belle Starr's Scalp," TROUBLED RANGE*; its "expansion," *CALAMITY, MARK AND BELLE*; *RANGELAND HERCULES*; *THE BAD BUNCH*; *Part Two, "We Hang Horse Thieves High," J.T.'S HUNDREDTH*; *THE GENTLE GIANT*; *Part Four, "A Lady Known As Belle," THE HARD RIDERS* and *GUNS IN THE NIGHT*. Belle also makes "guest" appearances in: *HELL IN THE PALO DURO*; *GO BACK TO HELL*; *THE QUEST FOR BOWIE'S BLADE* and *Part Six, Calamity Jane in "Mrs. Wild Bill," J.T.'S LADIES*.

2. Although Americans in general use the word "cinch" for the broad, short band made from coarsely woven horsehair, canvas, or cordage, and terminated at each end with a metal ring, which—together with the

"latigo"—is used to fasten the saddle on the back of a horse, because of its Spanish connotations, Texans employ the term "girth" and pronounce it, "girt." As Texans fastened the end of the rope to the saddlehorn when working cattle, or horses, instead of using a "dally" which could be slipped free in an emergency, their rigs had two girths for added security.

3. "Light a shuck": cowhands' expression for leaving hurriedly. It derives from the habit in night camps of trail drives and open range roundups of supplying "shucks"—dried corn cobs—to be used for illumination by anybody who had to leave the campfire and walk in the darkness. As the "shuck" burned away very quickly, a person had to move fast if wanting to benefit from its light.

4. "Make wolf bait": to kill. It derives from the practice in the Old West when a range was infested by predators—not necessarily wolves alone—of killing an animal, poisoning the carcass and leaving it to be devoured.

5. We suspect that the trend in film and television Westerns made since the early 1960s to portray all cowhands as long haired, bearded and filthy stems less from the desire of the production companies to create "realism" than because there were so few actors—to play supporting roles particularly—who were clean shaven and short haired and because the "liberal" elements who began to gain control of the entertainment industry appear to have an obsession for dirty conditions or filthy appearances. In our extensive reference library, we cannot find a dozen photographs of cowhands—as opposed to Army scouts, mountain men and old time gold prospectors—with long hair and bushy beards. In fact, our reading on the subject has led us to believe the term "long hair" was one of opprobrium in the Old West and Prohibition eras, as it is in cattle country today.

6. The sharp toes and high heels of the boots worn by cowhands were purely functional. The former could enter, or be slipped from, a stirrup iron very quickly in an emergency. Not only did the latter offer a firmer grip in the stirrup iron, they could be spiked into the ground to supply extra braking power when roping on foot.